THE WILDCAT

A KROYDON HILLS LEGACY NOVEL

PLAYING TO WIN
BOOK TWO

BELLA MATTHEWS

Copyright © 2023

Bella Matthews

All rights reserved. No part of this publication may be reproduced or transmitted by any means, electronic, mechanical, photocopying, recording or otherwise, without the prior permission of the publisher, except in the case of brief quotation embodied in the critical reviews and certain other noncommercial uses permitted by copyright law.

Without in any way limiting the author's exclusive rights under copyright, any use of this publication to "train" generative artificial intelligence (AI) technologies to generate text is expressly prohibited. The author reserves all rights to license uses of this work for generative AI training and development of machine learning language models.

This is a work of fiction, created without use of AI technology. Resemblance to actual persons, things, living or dead, locales or events is entirely coincidental. The author acknowledges the trademark status and trademark owners of various products referenced in this work of fiction, which have been used without permission. The publication/use of these trademarks is not authorized, associated with, or sponsored by the trademark owners.

This book contains mature themes and is only suitable for 18+ readers.

Editor: Dena Mastrogiovanni, Red Pen Editing

Cover Designer: Sarah Sentz, Enchanting Romance Designs

Photographer: Wander Aguiar

Model: Andrew Biernat

Interior Formatting: Brianna Cooper

SENSITIVE CONTENT

This book contains sensitive content that could be triggering.
Please see my website for a full list.

WWW.AUTHORBELLAMATTHEWS.COM

This book is dedicated to my father, who gave me my love of reading, football, and hockey. The world shines a little less brightly without him in it. Not sure he would have appreciated the sex, though.

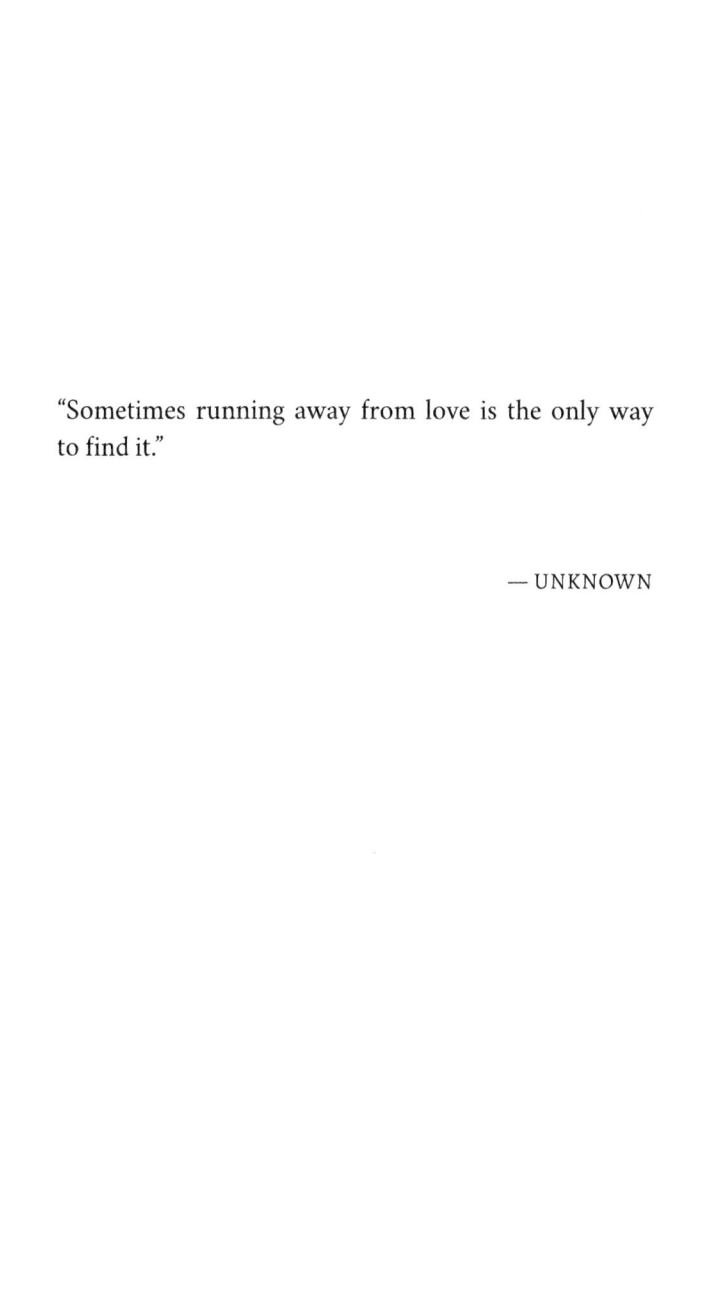

"Sometimes running away from love is the only way to find it."

— UNKNOWN

CAST OF CHARACTERS

The Kings Of Kroydon Hills Family

- **Declan & Annabelle Sinclair**
  - Everly Sinclair - 23
  - Grace Sinclair - 23
  - Nixon Sinclair - 22
  - Leo Sinclair - 21
  - Hendrix Sinclair - 18

- **Brady & Nattie Ryan**
  - Noah Ryan - 20
  - Lilah Ryan - 20
  - Dillan Ryan - 17
  - Asher Ryan - 11

- **Aiden & Sabrina Murphy**
  - Jameson Murphy -20
  - Finn Murphy - 17

- **Bash & Lenny Beneventi**
  - Maverick Beneventi - 20
  - Ryker Beneventi - 18

- **Cooper & Carys Sinclair**
  - Lincoln Sinclair - 13
  - Lochlan Sinclair - 13
  - Lexie Sinclair - 13

- **Coach Joe & Catherine Sinclair**
  - Callen Sinclair - 23

The Kingston Family

- **Ashlyn & Brandon Dixon**
    - Madeline Kingston - 24
    - Raven Dixon - 8

- **Max & Daphne Kingston**
    - Serena Kingston - 17

- **Scarlet Cade St. James**
    - Brynlee St. James - 23
    - Killian St. James - 21
    - Olivia St. James - 19

- **Becket & Juliette Kingston**
    - Easton Hayes - 28
    - Kenzie Hayes - 22
    - Blaise Kingston - 12

- **Sawyer & Wren Kingston**
    - Knox Kingston - 16
    - Crew Kingston - 13

- **Hudson & Maddie Kingston**
    - Teagan Kingston - 17
    - Aurora Kingston - 14
    - Brooklyn Kingston - 9

- **Amelia & Sam Beneventi**
    - Maddox Beneventi - 22
    - Caitlin Beneventi - 19
    - Roman Beneventi - 17

- Lucky Beneventi - 15

- **Lenny & Bash Beneventi**
  - Maverick Beneventi - 20
  - Ryker Beneventi - 18

- **Jace & India Kingston**
  - Cohen Kingston - 16
  - Saylor Kingston - 11
  - Atlas Kingston - 8
  - Asher Kingston - 8

For family trees, please visit my website www.authorbellamatthews.com

The Philly Press

KROYDON KRONICLES

SUMMER IN THE CITY

Holy hot summer, peeps. Have *ALL* the beautiful people fled to the beach for the Fourth of July and decided to stay there for the rest of the month? It's been awfully quiet in Kroydon Hills. Too quiet, if you ask me. And this reporter is bored. Time to find a little action. Stay tuned.
#KroydonKronicles #Hotgirlsummer

EVERLY

"What are you really doing here, evil spawn?" Maddox pushes my jalapeño margarita across the bar with a raised brow. "Your crew's not in the city."

I wrap my fingers around the stem of the glass, but he tugs it out of my hand and holds it hostage while he waits for an answer.

Asshole.

As if I don't know my best friends are all on vacation. My sister is touring the country on her first national ballet tour. And the rest of my family is at the beach. Without me.

Like I somehow could miraculously miss the fact that I'm alone.

"That's because Lindy, Kenzie, and Brynlee are on some tropical island with the rest of your family, and Gracie doesn't get home from her tour until next week." I yank the glass back and manage to only allow a smidge of jalapeño goodness to splash over the side. He's an ass, but he makes a damn good margarita. "Why aren't you on vacay with the rest of your family?" I push, kinda hoping sparring with

Maddox will make me feel a little less sorry for myself. I don't do pity parties. At least I don't like to. But I'm not sure even sparring with Madman will fix my funk.

Maybe the margarita will help.

I take a sip, savoring the cool, spicy goodness as it slips down my throat, hoping it dulls my sadness. I'd welcome a little reprieve any way I can get one. Pretty sure I'm getting on my own nerves now.

Not that I'll admit *any* of that to him.

Hell, I barely want to admit it to myself.

Maddox and I have been friends our entire lives. Our moms are best friends, who used to joke that the two of us were destined to be soulmates.

Seriously. Who talks like that?

Oh wait, my mom does because my dad and her have been disgustingly in love since the day they met. The kind of in love where they can't keep their hands off each other, and he still brings her flowers just because.

Umm . . . No, thank you.

And hell to the *no*, not with Maddox Beneventi. He's more like a brother to me than a *real* guy, and possibly an even bigger pain in my ass than my actual brothers, which is really saying something, considering the three of them are shitheads.

Madman wipes down the bar, then smacks me with the damp towel. "I'm skipping the island this year. Someone had to stay in town, so I told Dad I'd do it. Mom loves this stupid family vacation. I didn't want them to miss it."

"Aww, Madman. You're not going soft on me, are you?" I tease . . . and drink. And drink some more.

Tonight sucks.

Happy birthday to me.

"Not to worry, evil twin. Not a single inch of me is soft,

and there's a whole lotta inches." His wicked grin almost makes me gag. *Almost.*

"You're gross. Keep your inches to yourself." I swallow the rest of my drink, savoring the tequila, then nod toward my glass. "Refill, please."

"Going kinda fast, don't you think?" Maddox asks pointedly as he empties the rest of the shaker into the glass, then tosses a few little red pepper slices on top. "Might want to slow it down. I'm not carrying your tiny ass home."

"That happened one time, and you're never going to let me live that down, are you?"

He shakes his head, and my eye twitches.

"Whatever. Cut me a break. It's the first time in twenty-three years I haven't been with Gracie on our birthday. I haven't seen my sister in weeks, and my entire family is already at the beach compound. Much less glamorous than your family's entire island, but still, that's where everyone is. Which leaves me *here*, on my birthday . . . Alone . . . *With you*," I groan. "I don't want to spend my birthday with you, Maddox."

A deep, sexy, vibrating laugh comes from next to me, which pisses me off. I don't care how sexy it sounds. Nobody likes to be laughed at. Especially a woman indulging in a pity party on her birthday.

"Excuse me?" I turn my head enough to look at the person behind the deep, rumbly sound, then drag my eyes up . . . *And up*. And—oh wow—up some more, until I'm looking at a face. A devastatingly handsome face. *Damn*. Deep brown eyes, framed by thick black lashes most women would pay a fortune for, hold me locked in place. *Hostage*. As my brain momentarily short-circuits.

"That's okay. No excuse needed." The deep timbre of his voice is melodic and soothing in an annoying kind of way because I do not need to be soothed by a stranger.

I watch as he takes a pull from a beer bottle, then cracks a smile and . . . *Oh hell.* I think my panties just got wet. That smile is so sexy. The kind of smile that holds a cocky, confident promise of all the sinfully delicious things those lips could do.

Damn. I try to lock down those thoughts.

I'm not doing this. *That.* Him.

Nope. No strangers. Hell, no men. I'm detoxing from men. Men suck.

They're a distraction, and I don't need any of those.

"Oh . . ." I laugh. "That's cute. You think—" I laugh a little harder. A little more forced for his sake and maybe the sake of my dignity. "No. *Sorry* to disappoint, but I wasn't apologizing to you. I was apologizing *for* you. You see, I was taught eavesdropping on private conversations is rude. Obviously, you skipped the day manners were handed out growing up."

If it's possible, that damn smile grows a little bigger and a whole lot cockier. "Oh, darlin', I've never had anything handed to me. And my momma made sure I have excellent manners. She also taught me never to brag." He looks over at Maddox, who's moved on to the other end of the bar, where he's helping the co-eds who just came into West End. They're probably ordering some froufrou drink, hoping one of them will get to go home with him at the end of the night. "Real men don't need to brag. But hey, if you want to check out his hard inches, go right ahead."

He leans his head in conspiratorially toward mine and crooks his finger. "Fair warning, though. If a man's got to brag, he's usually full of shit."

Wow. He even smells good. Sandalwood and something else.

"Did you just sniff me?" he whispers, and I laugh. *Hard.* No force needed this time.

"Sorry. I've been on a bit of a cleanse. And you . . ." I bite down on my bottom lip. "Well, you're like a big old, tempting piece of chocolate cake."

For a second, he looks at me funny. Maybe he thinks I'm crazy.

At least, that's what it looks like to me.

But seriously, who am I to guess what a complete stranger is thinking?

I lean my elbow on the bar and rest my face in my hand. "Who are you?"

"According to you, I'm a piece of chocolate cake," he challenges with a fucking twinkle in his eye. Good lord, he's twinkling. It's like a neon sign screaming—*Stay away . . . Stay far away. Trouble ahead.* But I'm pretty sure I'd *really* enjoy his brand of trouble.

And like a moth to a flame, I think my wings are about to get scorched.

Cross

The bombshell in the little white sundress stabbing the pepper slices in her drink with a tiny little straw looks at me with vibrant turquoise eyes, a beautiful mix of green and blue. She drags her teeth over her pouty pink-glossed lip before she shakes her head slowly. Shiny long blonde hair falls in waves around her face. Thick and glossy and sliding over her bare shoulders. She looks like she belongs in a shampoo commercial. Or bent over my bed with that hair wrapped around my fist.

"Did I mention I love chocolate cake?" she murmurs, and I laugh. "I just know it's bad for me, so I'm trying to . . ."—she mulls something over for a minute, then smiles—

"*abstain* from cake. All desserts really . . . At least for the summer."

"Seems like a waste of a summer, if you ask me," I tell her, even though flirting with this woman is the last fucking thing in the world I should be doing.

She nods slowly. "I think you might be right."

The bartender with the *hard inches* and hard-on for the blonde, heads back our way and raps his knuckles against the bar. "Food should be up soon, man. Sorry about the wait."

"No problem." I watch the guy walk away, then look back to the bombshell next to me. "He your boyfriend?"

She runs her finger along the salty rim of her glass, then sucks it between her lips.

Fuck . . . No way she doesn't know what she's doing.

"No," she says slowly. "Just a friend. More like an annoying little brother who I'm not exactly related to."

I must make a face because she smiles and adds, "Let's just say my family is big. And mostly annoying. And Maddox belongs firmly in the family category."

"Good to know." I look down at my phone and see a text notification from my own annoying family. My brother, Ares, and I flipped a fucking coin to decide who had to pick up dinner tonight. I lost. Although, right about now, it feels more like maybe I won.

ARES

Dude. I'm fucking starving. Where's dinner?

BELLAMY

Why are you so dramatic? There's leftover Chinese food in the fridge if you're that hungry. Or you could try eating a piece of fruit. Or God forbid, a vegetable.

ARES

Listen little sister. Unless you want me to call Mom and tell her about the new guy you're seeing, I'd keep your opinions to yourself.

BELLAMY

It was one date. Like I said. DRAMATIC. I could always tell Mom about the bottle blonde that you were in the pool with last week. Her moans were almost as fake as her tits, Ares.

ARES

Those moans were real. Take it back.

BELLAMY

Quit kidding yourself.

CROSS

Do you think this is how Dad felt when you two used to fight?

ARES

Probably.

BELLAMY

Absolutely. Why do you think we both live with you now instead of him?

CROSS

Still waiting on the food. Not sure how long it's gonna be. Might want to eat the Chinese.

BELLAMY

Take your time. The kids are asleep. And Ares will survive. Maybe if we stop feeding him after sunset, he'll stop turning into an asshole. Kinda the opposite of a gremlin.

ARES

Fuck off. I'm hungry.

> **BELLAMY**
> You're always hungry.

> **CROSS**
> Jesus Christ. Remind me why you're both living with me?

> **BELLAMY**
> Because you love me.

> **ARES**
> Because you love the way I protect your ass on the ice.

I shake my head and shove my phone back in my pocket, smiling, then look up at the woman staring curiously at me. She's turned on her bar stool. Her bare legs crossed, and the delicate white cotton dress riding up perfect, creamy thighs.

Holy fucking hell.

"How old are you?" I ask because I'm pretty damn sure this girl is young. Not–*I'm a creep for looking*–young. But I've definitely got her beat by a few years.

Long black lashes kiss her cheeks as she takes another sip before she lifts her eyes to mine. "Old enough that my ID isn't fake."

Fuck . . . I like her attitude. Confidence is fucking sexy.

And this woman has confidence in spades.

"What exactly does your ID say?" I push back.

She pulls her little straw from her glass and points it at me like she's wielding a weapon. "You say your momma taught you manners, yet you still ask a lady how old she is." She tsks. "Shame. I bet she'd yell at you for that."

The straw goes back into the glass before she nails me with a single look, wraps her lips around the straw, and sucks. My dick comes alive in a way it hasn't in fucking months. In all reality, it's probably been closer to years. Ways it shouldn't with this girl.

"Does that ID say a name or am I just supposed to call you Cinderella all night? You gonna leave me your shoe before hopping in your pumpkin?"

A slow, pretty smile spreads across her face. "I was more of a Rapunzel fan. But I guess it'll do. Although Rapunzel had the hottest prince." She looks me up and down, and if it's possible, her smile grows even more dazzling. "Has anyone ever told you, you'd make a pretty good Flynn Rider?" She cocks her head to the side, assessing. "Maybe more the size of Kristoff though . . . Not that you know who they are, I'm sure."

I don't bother telling her I know every Disney prince and princess, thanks to my daughter, Kerrigan.

Who knew a three-year-old and a grown woman would have the same taste in movies?

"Shit," she mumbles, bringing me out of my thoughts and ducks her head.

I look around, but nothing looks off. "What's wrong?"

"No . . . *No*. No," she chants quietly, then leans in closer to me. Her sun-kissed skin nearly glows in the dim lighting, and warmth emanating from her pulls me in as her hand moves to grip the front of my t-shirt. "Listen, I know you don't know me, but I swear I'm not crazy," she whispers quickly.

"Not sure I buy that, but okay. You're not crazy." She is sure *driving* me crazy though.

Her delicious scent wraps around me, and my mouth waters.

Cherries dipped in vanilla, mixed with temptation.

A whole lot of temptation.

And I have to fight the overwhelming urge to touch her

when a lock of her soft hair slides forward and tickles the side of my face.

What the hell is it about this girl?

"I need you to be my boyfriend for five minutes."

"What—"

She pulls me closer, cutting me off. "I'm really sorry. But I'm going to kiss you now." The sentence comes out more like one long word as wild eyes plead for me to go with it.

What the—

She presses her lips against mine. Silky smooth and soft. They linger on mine long enough for me to get a hint of a taste. A tiny tease of a touch that doesn't satisfy anything. Then just as quickly, they're gone.

Over before it started, this crazy, beautiful blonde pulls back, giggling with her hand still clutching the front of my shirt.

From the outside, it probably looks like we were sharing a private joke.

In our own world.

Intimate.

And, *yeah* . . . I want in on that fucking joke and that fucking world.

I want more.

Out of the corner of my eye, I catch a guy about her age walking our way and nod toward him as I look at her. "*He* who the show's for?"

My little Cinderella leans in close again, her soft hair cascading down against me in a sheet of gold. "An ex who wanted more than I did and doesn't like to take no for an answer."

I give up the fight and tuck that damn lock of hair behind her ear, then let my fingers trail down the soft skin behind her ear and cup her neck.

I don't fucking like that answer. No is all any woman

should ever have to say to get a man to back the fuck off. Even if I have no doubt this girl is hard for a man to give up. But this dude doesn't look like a man. He looks like a pansy-ass college kid, who probably doesn't have a fucking clue where a clit is.

Dumb fucks like him are all about themselves. They don't have any idea how intoxicating it can be to make a woman fall apart in your arms. The sounds she makes while you're coaxing another from her. Or how fucking good the wait can be.

And without overthinking why, I slide my hand up the back of Cinderella's head and press my lips to hers. Fast and hard—like a heavy clap of thunder followed by a deafening crack of lightning—the fucking Earth shifts, and the noise from the busy bar fades into the background. I capture her mouth with mine, sliding my tongue against hers, and she fucking melts in my arms. Soft and pliant. Not at all what I was expecting from this little wildcat.

A sweet sigh slips past her lips as her hands slide up my chest and around my neck until long nails are digging into my scalp and tugging on my hair.

A throat clears to our right as a bag of food is dropped on the bar to my left, and a growl works it's way up my throat. I don't do audiences.

When I pull back, her hands slide to my shoulders, and her dark pupils are blown wide with want.

Neither of us acknowledge the douche next to us.

This is probably stupid.

Definitely impulsive.

Two things I don't do, but there's no fucking way I'm stopping now.

I already paid for the food, so I grab the handles of the bag and stand with my other hand out to her. "You want to get out of here?"

My own voice sounds thick with hunger, and I have no fucking clue what I'm doing...

But when she places her delicate hand in mine and smiles, I don't have a clue or a *care* because what I've got is the girl.

EVERLY

I follow my own growly anti-prince charming down the dimly lit hall, leading to the back door of West End . . . At least I follow until he apparently decides we're far enough away from the crowded bar and stops suddenly. He drops his bag of food to the floor and pins me against the rough wall, next to Maddox's office door.

I'm five five, and this man towers over me. His big chest and broad shoulders test the cotton of the soft, black t-shirt stretched around him, doing a lousy job of hiding a body I want to touch . . . To taste . . . To lick. Every. Last. Inch. Of. It.

I make the mistake of staring into his dark eyes as I try to remind myself I'm detoxing from men. *And this guy* . . . I bet this guy is *all man*.

His mouth hovers over mine as big hands press against the wall on either side of my face. Hands I want on my body. "Tell me you want this, Cinderella."

Cinderella?

I like it.

Two strangers.

Only we're not dancing at a ball.

Ever since I was a little girl, my ballerina mother has told my twin sister and me that we have matching black-and-white swans on our shoulders. Like little angel and devil ballerinas watching over us. Mom owns a dance studio where Gracie and I grew up. It wasn't hard to imagine our swans. And right now, my white swan is straightening her pristine tutu and fixing her perfectly slicked-back bun as she whispers, *No. Strangers are a hard no.*

I don't have too many hard no's. But she's right. Strangers are a hard no for me.

I swallow the lump of unimaginable want clawing its way up my throat and force strained words quietly past my lips. "I don't even know your name."

I hardly recognize my own voice.

He moves one powerful hand down to cup my face, and his calloused thumb skims over my jaw, sending electricity dancing along my skin. My nipples peak and strain against the bodice of my dress as all my synapses fire instantaneously. My body screams, *yes please*, while my brain short-circuits, and all thoughts of any type of cleanse go out the window.

My little black swan is kicking off her pointe shoes as she reminds me, *Rules are made to be broken.*

She might be right.

Can't imagine this is what Mom was thinking when she used to talk about them.

"Cross." My sexy stranger's voice caresses my skin, and I stare blankly back at him, my body shaking with anticipation, unable to process what he's telling me.

"My name . . ." A crooked, sinfully seductive smile curves his lips. "It's Cross."

My breath catches in my throat, and my rapidly beating heart skips a beat.

"Cross," I whisper back, liking the way that one word sounds on my lips. A sexy name for a sexy man.

I lean into his big body and run my finger along the stubble on his jaw. "Everly. Guess we're not strangers anymore."

His mouth crashes down over mine. Rough and hard and fucking perfect. Urgent. Like the idea of not kissing me is agonizing. And I get it because I don't think I've ever wanted anyone or *any* thing as much as I want this.

Need and want war with awareness.

Of *where* we are and *who* could see us.

But need and want win out.

Fuck awareness.

Cross grabs my ass in his big hands and lifts me from my feet. My legs are guided around his lean waist as he settles between my thighs, and *oh my*. It sure feels like everything is massive on this man. Sparks flicker behind my lids as a delicious ache grows deep inside me.

I wrap one arm around his neck and drop my other hand to the doorknob next to us and shove it open. Maddox may never forgive me, but I couldn't possibly care less.

With a crooked smile and one hand still on my ass, Cross pulls back, grabs the bag of food, and walks us through the door before he kicks it shut. "I'm not even going to ask how you know this room is here."

"Good." I reach behind him and flick the lock on the door. "Because I don't want to talk." My words come out thick and husky before Cross takes my mouth again and leans me back against the door.

One palm slides under my white cotton sundress and rough fingers dig into the flesh of my ass.

With shaky hands, I shove his shirt up and over his head, then drop it to the floor.

Oh. My. God.

This man's chest is chiseled steel.

His muscles ripple under my fingers between us as I coast them along his pecs and over his ridiculously ripped washboard abs.

"Like what you see?"

I tilt my head to the side and lick my lips as his dark eyes devour me. "I should have known you'd be cocky."

I don't tell him how much I like it.

That smile curves his lips as his finger skims along the seam of my lace thong, playing dangerously close to my clit. "*Arrogant*," he corrects me. "Not cocky."

"What's the—"

He slides his finger under my panties and pushes it inside me before I can question the difference and, *oh God* . . . I throw my head back and moan . . . loud and long and deep in my throat.

His mouth moves to my neck before he drags his tongue along my collarbone, licking and sucking and scraping his teeth along my hypersensitive skin. My toes curl, and my thighs tremble as I lock my ankles together and dig my heels into his solid ass.

My God. This man is solid . . . *everywhere*.

And what does he do? This sexy fucking man stuffs my pussy with two more fingers and curls them just . . . fucking . . . right. "Cocky men have to brag, sweetheart."

His warm breath fans my cool skin and goosebumps break out everywhere as he licks into my mouth, then teasingly bites down on my bottom lip. "Arrogant men know what they're capable of and don't worry about proving it. We just do it." His fingers pump in and out and curl again, hitting that sweet spot even my vibrator usually misses. And faster than I realize what's happening, my body shakes, and I come with a burst of light flashing behind my eyes.

Cross

She rides my hand like a fucking goddess.

A golden fucking goddess.

Golden-blonde hair. Warm sun-kissed skin. Her pretty, prim little sundress hides a body made for sin. And those fucking eyes . . . Green. And blue. The color of an angry ocean wave.

I pull my fingers from her cunt and drag them over her delicate collarbone, just under a dainty, gold necklace. I drag my tongue over the same spot before painting her lips with her own juices and sucking them between mine.

"Cross," she mewls against my lips. "Please tell me you have a condom . . ."

With one hand still holding her against the wall, I reach back and grab my wallet and a condom, then drop the wallet to the floor.

Everly reaches between us, unbuckles my jeans, and shoves them down under my ass, then shimmies until I drop her feet to the floor.

She presses her lips against my shoulder and bites down as she strokes my cock in her hand. One skinny strap of her sundress slips off her shoulder, hinting at tits I'd bet my last dollar are perfect. The muscles in my neck grow tight with the restraint I'm trying to hold onto like a fucking lifeline, so I don't bend this woman over and fuck her senseless.

Not that that's not going to happen. But I'm going to enjoy her first.

With hurried fingers, she tears the condom out of my

hand and rips the foil packet open with her teeth. Her lips curl into a sexy smile as she sheathes me, then strokes me. Long dark lashes flutter as she shrugs out of both skinny straps of her dress.

Hints of pretty pink nipples play peek-a-boo with the white fabric, and holy hell . . .

My words get stuck in my throat.

This woman. This fucking goddess . . .

"Everly . . ." I run my hands up her ribs and cup her perfect breasts in my hands.

Perfect handfuls.

Her eyes flash, and she turns her back to me and places her palms against the door before she looks over her shoulder at me. "Don't fall in love, Cross."

I drag my palms up her thighs, taking her dress with me.

Twin dimples pop deep in her cheeks. "Now fuck me."

Months from now, I'll probably look back and think this is where I should have ended the night. Should have gone home and kissed my kids and forgotten all about the golden-haired, sun-kissed goddess.

But hindsight's twenty-twenty.

And right now, I want to fuck this woman more than I want my next breath.

My hands run over the exquisite curve of her body.

The dip of her hips.

The flat of her stomach.

I drag my cock through her soaked sex and revel in the way her body shakes, then drop my lips to her ear. "You sure you want this?"

She drops her head against the door and arches back into me.

"I need your words, Cinderella."

"Yes." She trembles under my touch. "Please, God. Fuck me."

Not needing to be told twice, I wrap my hands around her hips and slide home until I bottom out inside her. "Fuck," I hiss as she cries out. It's the hottest sound I've ever heard.

I hold us still with the overwhelming fucking perfection of her body adjusting to mine before we move together. Skin on skin. Torturously slow at first but not for long. I wrap her glorious golden hair around my fist and pull her face back to mine. Our lips crash together. Tongues tangling in a furious, messy kiss. Sensations flood me. Ones I shouldn't be having.

Words press at my lips, wanting to be said.

Mine. Mine. Mine.

Words I have no business thinking.

Instead I suck her tongue and work her clit until she's screaming my name.

Even then, I keep fucking her, not willing to stop . . . not ready for this to be over.

"Give me another one, Everly." I pull out and turn her around, then boost her back up against the door and sink inside her wet heat. Her breasts bounce with each thrust of her hips, and her nails dig in, biting my skin.

"Oh, God. Cross," she whimpers, and I thrust harder. *Faster.* While, she chants my name over and over.

My lips cover hers. Swallowing her moans and my own.

Until she's shaking again. Tightening around me. Squeezing the life out of me, and I'm crashing into oblivion, filling the fucking condom between us.

Everly clings to me, her dress a rumpled mess between us. Her lips press against my damp skin, and her tongue licking the column of my neck, tasting me.

I don't put her down. Not yet.

I don't want the bubble to burst.

But I don't have much choice when a heavy bang on the door threatens to kick it in.

"Evil twin. You'd better not be fucking in my office," the furious voice shouts.

And what does my sun-kissed goddess do?

Her curls tumble over her shoulder as she turns and smiles at me. "Guess we should have been faster."

Fuck.

I gently place Everly down on unsteady feet and step back like a fucking high-school kid who just got caught in the back of my dad's truck for the first time. "Let me guess . . . The guy behind the bar?"

This girl doesn't even blush as she watches me pull up my jeans. She just bites down on her bottom lip before a giggle slips out with the next bang. "Chill out, Madman. I'll be out in a sec."

My eye twitches. "Madman?"

"I told you. Little brother. Not boyfriend. Don't go getting all upset now, big man." She adjusts her dress, then lifts up on her toes and kisses my cheek. "Maybe I'll see you around, Cross."

I wrap a hand around her head and drag her back to me for another kiss . . . and there she goes melting against me again. "Yeah. You can bet on that." I pull my phone from my pocket and hold it out for her. "How about you give me your number?"

She cocks a brow, then takes the phone from my hand. Her thumbs fly across the screen before her own phone beeps in her pocket. With a coy smile, she does the same to her own phone, then waves. "Bye, Cross."

I watch her quietly as she slinks through the door without looking back, then glance down at my phone.

CINDERELLA

I left you a shoe. Let's see if you can find me.

Sure enough, her shoe sits on the floor next to my food.
What the hell did I just do?

CROSS

"What took so long?" Ares bitches from where he's lying on the couch when I walk into my house. He kills the last of whatever he's shooting on his video game before popping up. "I'm starving."

I drop the West End bag down on the table and ignore my younger brother, not in the mood for his bullshit. Not when my thoughts keep going back to my sun-kissed Cinderella.

Find me...

Damn.

"You survived, didn't you?" I grab a beer from the fridge and watch Ares beeline to the food like a feral fucking dog that hasn't eaten in a month. "You know you don't have to bulk *that* much over the summer, right?" I rib him.

He eats more than any player I know. He always has. Ares moved in a few months ago, after he was traded to the Philadelphia Revolution mid-season last year. I always hoped he and I would get to play hockey together again but didn't realize that would mean living with him again too. I mean, I moved out when I started playing in the juniors at eighteen.

It's been well over a decade since we've lived under the same roof. At least now we don't share a room.

"Fuck off, asshole. You don't want me wasting away when I'm kicking someone's ass for you on the ice, do ya?" he mocks and sorts through the food.

"Whatever. Where's Bellamy?"

The only way Mom and Dad would let our sister go to college away from them was if she was near one of us. She picked me and chose Kroydon University. Smart kid.

She just finished her first year studying to be an RN. She spent a lot of time in hospitals in high school. Pretty sure that influenced her career.

It definitely fucked with everyone around her, me included.

When you come so close to losing someone you love at such a young age, it puts things in perspective. *Quickly.*

Bellamy's a handful with a heart of gold, and she's got Ares and me wrapped around her little finger. Always has.

"Dude . . ." He pulls all the food out and looks at me. "This shit's cold."

"Fuck off." I smile. "I drove and paid for it. Next time, get it yourself."

Guess my good mood from earlier soured during the drive home.

I blame the shoe.

That stupid, goddamned shoe.

I don't play games. I haven't in a really long time. The fact I'm considering it for this girl blows my mind. My ex was the one who liked to play games. She did it often . . . too often.

Enough for the both of us, no matter how much she knew I hated it.

Helene and I hooked up after a hockey game a few years ago. One weekend turned into two. Two weekends turned into a month, and before we hit two months, she was pregnant with my daughter, Kerrigan. I tried to do the right thing but couldn't bring myself to marry her. Not when I knew I didn't love her. Not then. Not yet. Turned out, not ever.

We moved in together and tried to make it work for Kerrigan's sake, but pretty fucking quickly, it was easy to see she wasn't made to be a mother. Helene was more interested in being the wife of a professional athlete and living the lifestyle that goes with it, more than she was in our daughter. She pushed for a ring. For a wedding. For a title. She never actually pushed for the marriage or the relationship.

I love Kerrigan with all my heart, and Helene gave me her, so I tried to make it work for my baby girl, which was more than she ever did. Everything else took priority over our family.

She was supposed to be on the pill when she got pregnant with our son, Jaxon, nearly two years after Kerrigan was born. I think she thought I'd have no choice but to marry her then. When it became obvious it wasn't going to work, instead of trying to figure it out, Helene threw a fit and left. A lawyer reached out to me a few weeks later and offered me full custody of the kids if I gave her a settlement like she'd get in a divorce. I jumped at the chance. She signed away all legal rights, and I haven't looked back.

That was months ago, and I haven't seen or heard from her since.

I also hadn't had sex since either.

Until tonight.

Until Everly.

Fuck . . .

I grab Ares's hand just as his fingers snap in front of my face. "Knock it off, asshole."

"What the hell's wrong with you?"

"Nothing." I shake my head and walk away.

Bellamy brushes past me, then stops. "Hey," she quirks her brow. "Where are you going?"

"To take a shower," I groan.

She tilts her head to the side and stares intently, like she's trying to find the missing piece of a puzzle. "Why? Did you get dirty picking up dinner?"

"Drop it, Bellamy," I warn, but that piques her interest even more, and she looks over at Ares. "What crawled up his butt?"

Dumb ass shrugs as a glob of ketchup from his burger drips out of his mouth.

"Oh my God. Mom would die if she saw you eating like that." Bellamy cringes before focusing her attention back on me. "Fine. Go shower. The kids are asleep. Kerrigan is super excited to go see Grandma and Grandpa this weekend. Two days left to cross off on her calendar. And she may have convinced me to help her pack already. Are we sure she's three and not thirteen?" She grabs a quesadilla from the table and moans as she bites into the cheese-filled triangle.

"Wait." Ares looks up from inhaling his food. "Is that it? Not in the mood to go back to Maine?"

I shrug, not sure what the hell's wrong with me. "I don't know. Just in a shit mood. I'm gonna shower. Don't eat my fucking sandwich."

This time when I walk away, no one stops me.

> **CROSS**
>
> My sister got in my car this morning and wanted to know why I have a woman's espadrille in my front seat. I didn't know what the hell an espadrille was. But she informed me the one in my car was a very expensive one and maybe I should give it back to its owner.

> **CINDERELLA**
>
> Well hello to you too, big man. An espadrille is a summer shoe that I happen to love. They're versatile.

> **CROSS**
>
> They're a shoe.

> **CINDERELLA**
>
> Oh, you poor obviously less than fashion educated man.

> **CROSS**
>
> Guess I missed that class growing up too. How many shoes do you need?

> **CINDERELLA**
>
> Shoes and chocolate, Cross. You can never have too much of either.

> **CROSS**
>
> Do you want yours back?

> **CINDERELLA**
>
> Maybe . . .

This girl . . . what is it about her? How can sexy come across in a text message?

And why do I need to know more?

Like she's my drug of choice, and I'm dying for my next hit.

CROSS

Tell me something about yourself.

CINDERELLA

I'm a twin, and this is the first time my sister and I haven't been together for our birthday . . . ever.

CROSS

Happy birthday.

CINDERELLA

It was last night.

CROSS

Pretty sure I gave you your present then.

CINDERELLA

Yeah, you did.

CROSS

Why were you alone if it was your birthday?

CINDERELLA

My family is on vacation but I had to work. My friends are all off enjoying the sun and sand too. We'll do something when they all get back and Gracie comes home.

CROSS

Your sister?

CINDERELLA

Yup. One sister. Three brothers. How about you?

CROSS

One brother. One sister.

I debate my next text.

I haven't dated since Kerrigan was born.

Hell, I haven't flirted with anyone but her mother in four years.

Haven't even wanted to until now.

Until Everly.

CINDERELLA
Think you can find me yet?

CROSS
Based off the fact you have four siblings? Probably not.

CINDERELLA
Okay, you can ask one more question today.

CROSS
Do you like playing games, Everly?

CINDERELLA
No, Cross. I like having fun.

I want to have more fun with you.

Will that help you find me?

CROSS
I didn't realize I had homework.

CINDERELLA
I'm worth it.

I'm worth it.

The words play on repeat in my mind the rest of the day.

So does the hour I spent with her a few nights ago.

Her face . . . her smile . . . her laugh and smell . . . she's been burned into my brain.

I'm worth it.

I don't just see the words on my phone, I hear them in her voice.

How is it possible, after one damn night, that I don't doubt she is worth it?

A few days after my night at West End, my entire family is together at our parent's house in Kennebunkport, Maine, relaxing while we breathe in the fresh salt air and get doted on by Mom. All is right in Mary Jo Wilder's world when her entire family is under one roof.

Not gonna lie, my world feels lighter here too. Easier. It always has.

Words I don't usually associate with my life, but somehow just fit as I sit in one of Mom's rocking chairs on the front porch. My five-month-old, Jax, sleeps, content in my arms.

The sunset dots the horizon over the Atlantic Ocean in the distance and reminds me of summers as a kid. It's calm and quiet and somehow makes it easier to put the past year into perspective.

"Want some company?" Dad asks as he soundlessly closes the screen door behind him so he doesn't wake Jax and eyes the white rocker next to me.

"Your house, old man."

"That it is, Cross." Dad's smile stretches across his weathered face. "You've been quiet since you got here. Want to talk about it?"

I kiss the top of Jax's head and close my eyes, taking it all in. "Just thinking about life, Dad. Didn't exactly turn out the way I expected."

Dad chuckles. "It never does, son. But you've got plenty of time, and a pretty damn good life. You've got a beautiful family. A job you love. Money in the bank. Safety. Security. Don't be ungrateful, Cross."

My lips pull up. "I know I'm a lucky son of a bitch. I'm not complaining. Just thinking."

"Who's the girl?"

My chest vibrates with silent laughter, waking Jax, who buries his head in my neck. I rub his back with my palm until he settles, then glance at my father. "How do you know there's a girl?"

"There's always a girl."

I shrug, and the old man shakes his head. "You forget I was your age once."

"Thinking maybe I should swear off women for a while. Too complicated."

Dad crinkles his eyes. "They're all complicated. The key is to find one who's worth figuring out. Swear off women like Helene... sure. But not all women are like her, Cross. You've got to find a good one. Find the one who makes you a better man."

"Not everyone gets to have what you and Mom have." I kiss the top of Jax's head, and inhale.

"If you swear off women, you'll never have the chance, son. I had no idea your mother would turn out to be the love of my life, the night I met her. But she was worth the risk. Now look at us." He leans forward and tugs the blanket up Jax's back.

"Still a know it all?" I tease the old man.

He cracks a perceptive smile. "At least we know Ares comes by it honestly. Now tell me who you're thinking about."

I continue silently rocking without looking away.

"Fine. Tell me what's holding you back," Dad nudges,

making me feel like a fifteen-year-old afraid to tell him I like Chrissy Miller.

"I met her the other night, and there was something about her. But she's . . ." I chew on it for a minute, trying to figure out what's holding me back. "She's young. And beautiful. And . . . fun."

Dad makes a disgusted face. "Well damn, Cross. Nobody wants young and pretty and fun. That sounds like a miserable woman to date."

"Whatever, old man," I laugh.

"Did you get this girl's number?"

"Yeah, Dad. I got her number," I mumble.

"He got her shoe too, Daddy," Bellamy adds as she walks through the door and lets it slam shut behind her, startling Jax.

"Big mouth," I call after her as she skips down the steps and climbs into Mom's car.

"Be safe," Dad yells after her and watches her pull away before looking back at me. "A shoe, huh?"

I nod.

"Call the girl, Cross. A girl doesn't leave a shoe if she doesn't want to be chased."

I stand and sway, trying to calm Jax. "I don't like games, Dad."

"Games can be fun with the right person."

"Oh my God," I groan. "I don't need to hear that."

He stands and takes Jax from my arms. "Call the girl."

I watch as he disappears back into the house, then pull out my cell phone. A quick google search of her phone number comes back with the name Everly Sinclair. *Sinclair* . . . That name . . .

Why does that name sound familiar?

An hour later, I feel like I've gotten a master's degree in social-media stalking.

Everly Sinclair—social-media darling and aspiring fashion designer, according to the Kroydon Kronicles. Professional cheerleader for the Philadelphia Kings. Currently working for her aunt, Carys Sinclair, at a boutique in Kroydon Hills. She's young. *Twenty-three*. Eight years younger than me.

Eight years.

Damn . . .

Her twenties haven't even kicked her ass yet at twenty-three.

No wonder she's having so much fun.

I flip my phone over in my hand, debating my next move when Kerrigan and my mom come outside with a cherry pie in their hands. "Look what we made for you, Daddy."

I scoop my baby up in my arms and break off a piece of sugar-coated crust before my mom smacks my hand. "This is delicious."

Cherries always are.

Kerrigan smooshes my cheeks with her hands. "Don't talk with your mouth full, Daddy."

"Come on, baby. Let's go split a piece of pie." Kerrigan squeals when we stop and kiss Grandma. And that sound . . . that sound makes me happier than anything else ever will.

I stuff my phone in my back pocket and force myself to *try* to forget about Everly Sinclair . . . At least for now.

CROSS

> Everly Sinclair is a pretty name, but I still think Cinderella fits you better.

CINDERELLA

> Took you long enough.

CROSS

It's barely been a week.

CINDERELLA

I didn't have you pegged as slow, Cross.

CROSS

Some things are better slow, Cinderella.

CINDERELLA

Agree to disagree.

CROSS

Maybe I'll have to show you just how fun slow can be.

Okay, so maybe this flirting thing is like riding a bike. Muscle memory.

CINDERELLA

I wouldn't say no to that.

CROSS

Go out with me.

CINDERELLA

Was that supposed to be a question?

CROSS

Not really.

CINDERELLA

. . .

CROSS

How about we make a deal . . . I'll always tell you what I want and you can decide if that's what you want. I'm not into games.

CINDERELLA

I guess I can do that.

CROSS

I'm home in two weeks. Let me take you out.

CINDERELLA

Where are you?

CROSS

Visiting my family in Maine.

CINDERELLA

Oh. I'm on a USO tour in two weeks.

CROSS

That sounds cool.

CINDERELLA

It's actually a lot of fun. I cheer for the Philadelphia Kings. We do this every year before the season starts. But if you did your homework, you probably already knew that.

CROSS

Is football your favorite sport?

CINDERELLA

It's kind of a family tradition that my brothers screwed up by playing hockey instead. But in my opinion, football will always be the better sport.

CROSS

And why is that?

CINDERELLA

Some things just are. Why? Are you a hockey fan?

CROSS

You could say that.

THE WILDCAT

CINDERELLA

Maybe you'll come to one of the games and I can show you the error of your ways.

CROSS

Maybe I will.

CINDERELLA

Gotta go. Sweet dreams, Cross.

I'm sure they will be with a new picture of Everly in a Kings cheerleaders' uniform now burned into my brain.

The Philly Press

KROYDON KRONICLES

PUMPKIN LATTES & PRETTY PLAYERS

This reporter has never been so glad for summer in the city to come to an end. Hello fall. Bring on falling leaves, pumpkin lattes, and football players. Speaking of players . . . Kroydon Hills's favorite Kings player was caught canoodling with a buxom brunette last night in a tiny tavern just outside the city. Could this mystery girl be the one who finally catches Callen Sinclair, or is she just another fumble? Only time will tell . . . well, time and this reporter. Stay tuned #KroydonKronicles

EVERLY

"Ooh . . . that candle smells like Fireball," I tease as I sit down on the couch next to Lindy and happily steal a sleeping Griffin from her arms. This little man made his debut a few weeks earlier than any of us expected, and I may have lost a piece of my heart the day he was born. He's only two weeks old, but I think he's my new favorite person in the world.

"Hey, evil twin . . . Us non-alcoholics like to call that smell cinnamon," Callen mocks me from across the room.

Lindy throws a pillow at Callen. "Didn't know you were so up on your spices, manwhore."

"Whatever. My mom used to make cinnamon toast. I like cinnamon. Leave me alone," he fights back.

"Watch it, Callen, or I'll tell Grandpa why you were really late to practice last week." Grace flicks his ear for me. Uncle or not, Callen is only a week older than Grace and me, and we were all raised together. Torturing each other is basically our love language.

Our family is made up of actual family as much as friends

we've chosen as family. We're basically a mess. An annoying mess, but I wouldn't change it for the world.

"You wouldn't," Callen mocks Grace, and she smiles back at him.

"Man, I missed you, Grace." I run the tip of my finger down the length of Griffin's nose and enjoy the way his tiny hands ball into tight little fists.

Tonight's the first time my friends have all been in one place since Grace left for her tour at the beginning of the year. It did so well, they ended up extending it, and she only got back yesterday.

Lindy's husband, Easton, walks in with Maddox a minute later, carrying enough pizza boxes to feed a small village. "Did you get—"

"Yes, princess. I got your pineapple and ham pie," Easton tells Lindy before she can finish her sentence. He opens that box first and hands her a piece.

"Dude, trouble," Maddox groans. "That's fucking disgusting."

"Be nice," Kenzie, Easton's sister and one of my roommates, chides.

Maddox raises his brow. "I thought the pregnancy cravings were supposed to stop after the baby was born."

"And I thought you were smart enough not to question a hormonal woman. Looks like we're all wrong," Brynlee, my other roommate snaps.

Grace sighs happily. "Yup. This is what I missed."

Lindy lived with Grace, Kenzie, Brynlee, and me before she married Easton. Lucky for us, she only moved one floor down when she moved out.

"The fighting?" Kenzie questions, and Grace shakes her head.

"No. The family. Being here. Not having to hear about everything through a text." She smiles. "I even missed you,

Maddox." She leans her head back on the couch and looks up at Madman, who's staring down at her, *smiling*. Because that's the reaction Grace gets from everyone. "I want to hear about everything." She sighs wistfully.

Callen groans, and Madman smacks the back of his head.

I laugh, and Grace carefully steals Griffin from me. "Callen's just pissed he got caught banging that model the other night." I love picking on Callen. He just makes himself such an easy target. "The Kroydon Kronicles want to know if you're off the market."

"Whatever." He throws a piece of pepperoni at my face. "Did you tell Grace about getting caught banging the bar guy in West End, evil twin?"

"Hey." Lindy snatches the pepperoni and points at Callen. "No throwing meat near the baby."

"Pro athlete, Lindy. The pepperoni wasn't going near Griffin," Callen protests.

Embarrassment mixes with hot fucking memories as I picture my night with Cross at West End.

The man has starred in every daydream I've had since that night two months ago.

Grace nails me with excited eyes, a mirror image of my own. "Wait. Back up. She must have left that out." She slides her legs underneath herself on the couch and perks up as the rest of the girls snicker. "Bar guy, huh? I thought this was the summer of the cleanse, sissy."

I roll my eyes. "Stop . . . It was a lapse in judgment. I'd basically been off . . . *sugar* . . . for weeks. And he was like . . . Well, he was a big piece of triple chocolate fudge cake from Sweet Temptations bakery."

"Ohhh, yes," Lindy practically moans. "Easton," she calls to her husband, who's moved into the kitchen.

"Already stopped and got cupcakes, princess," he calls back.

Lindy hums happily, then looks around at all of us. "Shut up."

"I want to hear more about the sex at West End," Grace pushes, and I sink further into the couch.

"What do you want to know, Grace? How Everly banged the dude against. My. Fucking. Door. While I pounded on it with my fist because she locked me out? Of. My. Fucking. Office." Maddox groans. "Or what about how she walked out barefoot?"

"Not letting that go, huh?" I play it off, refusing to be embarrassed.

"Barefoot? What?" Grace giggles and bites down on her lip. "You're so lucky he didn't walk in."

I can't help my blush as I admit, "I locked the door."

"I'm the one who's lucky," Maddox groans. "Fuck. I don't need to see evil twin naked. I'd never be able to look at my office again. I've got to work in there." Maddox takes the beer Easton hands him on his way over to his wife and shakes his head. "Not like I've seen you guys together since that night either."

"Ohh . . . Why not?" Grace pushes, and I feel my blush deepen.

"Bad timing," I tell them. "He was out of town for a few weeks, then I had the USO thing."

"You're home now . . ." Lindy pushes.

"I am." I stand, wanting to get a slice of pizza... and maybe to get away from this conversation. "But I guess I was using the time away to reset my cleanse," I admit sheepishly before making my way to the kitchen.

I've got a slice of roasted garlic white pizza on my plate when Grace walks in behind me. She grabs a bottle of water and pulls herself up onto the counter, looking like my mirror image. Twins run in my family. There're a few sets. But Grace and I are the only identical twins. Mom always called us mirror twins because I have a tiny birthmark on my right cheek and Grace has one on her left. It's the only way people that don't know us can easily tell us apart. "So. Why haven't you told me about him?"

"There's nothing to tell." I take a bite of the garlicky goodness and watch her watching me. "What?"

Her eyes crinkle like she's sussing out a secret. "You like him."

"I've only seen him that one time . . ." I protest.

"Uh-huh. Lie to yourself if you want to, sissy. But you know you can't lie to me. You like this guy. You want to see him again."

Damn her for always being so observant.

I gently shrug. "Maybe."

"Have you talked to him since then?" She moves next to me and takes a bite of my pizza. "Man, I forgot how good the pizza from Milano's is."

I hand her my plate and grab another one. "Good. Eat a slice. You look like you've lost weight."

She hums around another bite. "Don't change the subject, Evie."

"Fine. I haven't talked to him, but we do text." I fidget for a second, then take a bite, buying myself time. "We've kept it kind of superficial though."

"What do you mean?"

I think back to the few conversations we've had. "Cross is good at asking questions. I've . . . Well, I've kind of left it up to him."

"You haven't asked him about himself? Why not?" She tilts her head, then places her plate on the counter and links her pinky with mine. "You know not all guys are going to hurt you the way Keith did, right?"

At the mention of my ex, my hackles raise. We spent the better part of three years doing the on-again-off-again thing.

He was there the night I met Cross. He was the reason for my cleanse. Then Cross happened. "I know. And I think this guy may be different . . ."

"But?" my sister pushes harder.

"But . . . I'm not sure yet."

Grace smiles back at me. "Okay. We'll put a pin in this for now. So . . . I need a favor."

"You just got home. What could you possibly need?"

She grimaces. "Listen, Mom asked me if I'd teach the Saturday morning baby ballerina class that starts tomorrow."

"Sucks to be you." I laugh until I see her face. "Oh, come on."

We've both taught classes at Hart & Soul, Mom's studio, for half our lives. But that doesn't mean I want to be doing it at twenty-three.

"Evie . . . I need some time off. I need a minute before I put my pointe shoes back on," she pleads.

"You don't need pointe shoes for toddlers, Grace. Come on. I dance every night of the week at cheer practice."

Grace pouts, and I give in immediately.

Her pout is evil.

She's the white swan.

I'm the black swan.

That's how it's always been.

I knew the minute she asked, I'd say yes.

"Fine. What time do I have to be there?"

Her eyes light up. "Class starts at nine."

Nine a.m. on a Saturday. "You owe me."

She brings our pinkies up between us. "Anything."

Famous last words.

THE WILDCAT

"What are you doing here, honey?" Mom asks from the front desk as I push through the door of Hart & Soul the next morning. "I thought your sister was teaching this class."

I shoulder my dance bag and move through the lobby we've affectionately dubbed *the fishbowl* because the parents can sit and watch their kids dance in the studio through a window in the room. Once I'm next to Mom, she kisses my cheek and fixes my bun. I hand her one of the two coffees I picked up next door at Maddox's mom's bakery, Sweet Temptations.

"Bless you," she mumbles as she greedily grabs her favorite coffee from me and sips. Annabelle Sinclair is a beautiful woman. She may be in her early forties, but she doesn't look a day over thirty, and I thank God for her good genetics often. A former prima ballerina who came back to town when her parents died, she became my Uncle Tommy's legal guardian, and lucky for my brothers, Grace, and me, she fell in love with our dad. She's also a saint.

Grace and I were never easy.

Well . . . I wasn't. Grace just got lumped in because of the whole twin thing. But my three younger brothers made us look like angels. They're hell on skates. All three of them. Much to my father's disappointment. Everyone always joked that Mom and Dad would end up with their very own football team. Instead, all three boys play hockey. Poor Dad.

Mom cups my cheek. "Go get changed, Evie. The girls should start arriving soon."

"What's the age range?" I call back as I head back to her office.

"Three and four today. Babies," I hear her answer before I shut her door and kick off my Uggs and sweats. I slip on my black skirt over my tights and adjust my pink sweater. Gotta look the part. A few bobby pins jammed into my bun or more accurately, my skull, later—because if it doesn't hurt, that sucker isn't staying put—and I'm ready to go. Or as ready as I'm going to be this early on a Saturday.

The sound of excited little girls greets me as I open the office door and step into the hallway, and I reach back into the office and grab my coffee. It's going to be a long day.

I walk out front and into the first studio, then turn on Mom's playlist for the baby ballerinas and stretch out a little. Not like I'm going to really be dancing, but muscle memory insists on it. I chug the final sip of my coffee and paste a smile on my face before shoving my shoulders back and walking into the fishbowl to greet the babies.

But when a tall, dark, and handsome man is standing there holding the hand of a baby ballerina, my words get stuck in my throat.

That handsome man holding the hand of a little girl in a pink tutu, who looks horrifically nervous, hasn't noticed me because he's squatting down in front of the little girl. Her blonde curls are already breaking free from her bun, and she's clutching a pink bunny to her chest. I stand there, entranced, watching Cross whisper something to the girl and then kiss her forehead as she nods in agreement.

Her little eyes move to me when he stands, and I smile and squat the way he just was. "Hi. My name is Miss Everly. What's your name?"

Big blue eyes look from me to her father, who stares at me like he just saw a ghost before he places his big palm on her small back. "Go ahead, baby. Tell her your name."

Oh. My. Goodness.

Can an ovary explode?

And if so, why the fuck did mine?

I've never had a daddy fetish.

The little girl looks at him again, and he nods, prompting her.

"Kerrigan," she whispers and grabs hold of Cross's leg.

I offer her my hand, and she takes it hesitantly. "Are you ready to have some fun, Kerrigan?"

She nods her little head, and her bun bobbles in place as Cross's eyes finally lock with mine. "You're welcome to have a seat over there and watch the class, Mr. . . ." Guess I should have asked Cross his last name before today.

"Wilder," he offers, and I smile.

"See you after class, Mr. Wilder."

Kerrigan turns around and hands the pink bunny to Cross. "Bye, Daddy."

Guess that answers that question.

I really should have asked more questions.

CROSS

I suck in an audible breath as if an invisible fist just sucker punched me, while my daughter walks through the door to an open dance studio, holding Everly Sinclair's hand.

Everly Sinclair.

My Cinderella.

Holding Kerrigan's hand.

Kerrigan, who doesn't like strangers. Who hates new people and places. Who I had to bribe to take ballet lessons with promises of a pink leotard and a stop at the bakery next door for cookies and whipped-cream-covered hot cocoa.

I rock back on my heels and force down the lump forming in my throat as my two worlds collide. My kids haven't come up in the little time Everly and I have found to text since that night at West End. Her teaching dance here somehow didn't manage to come up either.

Fuuuuck. I'm so fucking out of practice when it comes to the whole dating thing.

I haven't even gotten her to agree to a damn date yet.

Was I supposed to tell her about my kids already?

"It's okay, Mr. Wilder. *Your* daughter is in good hands with *my daughter*," a woman standing behind a desk next to me says matter-of-factly.

I turn to face her and am met with a slightly older version of Everly. I've seen pictures of her online, and they don't do her justice. Warm caramel-blonde hair is pulled back from her face, framing wide, green eyes. Eyes that are currently studying me curiously as she offers me her hand. "Annabelle Sinclair. Nice to meet you."

My hand dwarfs hers as we shake. "Cross Wilder. Nice to meet you, Mrs. Sinclair." Jesus. I'm reverting back to a teenage boy talking to his girlfriend's mom. Only that woman in the other room isn't my girlfriend. *No.* Everly is a skittish little thing. At first glance, she doesn't seem like she would be. But first glances would be wrong. She wants to see me again. I know it. But getting her to agree to it . . . Well, that's been harder than I expected.

A lesser man would step away.

Less sure of himself. Less sure of what he wants. Less willing to put in the work.

But I'm no lesser man.

I know what I want, and it's on the other side of that window.

Another parent moves in front of the desk to talk to Annabelle, and I'm cautiously relieved to be out of the hot seat, like an intimidated fucking teenager. *What the hell?* Something about the way she looked at me set my nerves on edge . . . Like she knew something. But she couldn't have . . .

No way Cinderella told her about that night, right?

Girls don't talk to their moms about guys they meet in bars, do they?

I look through the window at the room full of little girls, all with their eyes glued to the woman standing front and center. Her golden hair is pulled up into a bun. A much better one than what I managed this morning.

I'm going to need Bellamy's help next time.

Whatever Everly is saying has the little girls giggling in unison, and her cheeks flushing a pretty shade of pink.

Damn. She's gorgeous.

A gorgeous enigma.

She looks so damn sweet and innocent in front of them all, in her fuzzy pink sweater and that little black skirt barely covering her perfect ass. An ass I had in my hands.

Miss Evie seems much more sweet and innocent than the woman I met.

The one I'd like to get to know better. If she'd just let me.

Before I realize it, the class is over, and Kerrigan runs out of the room in a stampede of little girls, making a beeline directly toward me. "Daddy . . . Did you see me?" she asks softly. Always softly. I'm not sure my baby girl knows how to be loud.

I squat down to her level and cup her small shoulders in my hands. "I did see you. You did so good. Did you have fun?"

She nods her head up and down dramatically as Everly walks into the waiting room and claps her hands. "You all did so well today. Make sure to practice what I showed you, and we'll see you back here next Saturday."

Some parents stop to talk to Annabelle before they leave the studio, while others make their way over to Everly. It's easy to see why. There's something about her that's magnetic, like she's the sun and everyone else is lucky to orbit around her.

But for some reason, instead of focusing on any of them, her mischievous eyes find mine and hold . . . It's just for a moment before they drop down to Kerrigan and soften as a small smile tugs at her lips. I pick Kerrigan up and sit her on my hip and turn to Annabelle. "Say goodbye to Mrs. Sinclair, baby."

"Bye," barely leaves her lips before she tucks her face into my neck to hide.

"Bye, sweet girl. I'll see you next week," Annabelle tells her with her own mischievous look that reminds me of her daughter.

"You ready for your cookie?" I ask.

"And cocoa?" Kerrigan asks, perking up.

"Can't have cookies without cocoa, now can you?" Everly adds as she moves next to us. "Are you going to Sweet Temptations?"

"Yeah. That was our deal. Kerrigan would try something new, and then we'd get cookies after." I wonder if bribery makes me a shit dad.

"I used to bribe the girls with cupcakes all the time," Annabelle tells me, as if reading my mind. "It was the only way to get them to do anything for years." she laughs softly. "Guess some things never change."

"I blame you for my sweet tooth." Everly smiles back at her mother, who simply shrugs in her defense.

Kerrigan looks curiously from Everly to Annabelle. "Cupcakes?"

"Oh, yes." Annabelle nods. "The owner is one of my very best friends, and she makes the most delicious cupcakes in all of Kroydon Hills." Then she leans in closer and lowers her voice. "You can ask to taste them too."

Kerrigan's eyes grow wide with excitement before they turn to me. "Can we, Daddy?"

"Everly," her mother says. "Why don't you go with them and show Kerrigan what your favorite cupcake is."

"Mom," Everly cuts her mother off, but Annabelle has already planted the seed, and I swear to God, I think she just winked at me too.

Kerrigan cups her hands around my ear. "Can she come wif us, please?"

Everly flushes because for one of the first times ever, Kerrigan fails at being quiet.

I kiss my daughter's cheek and flash a smile at her pretty dance teacher. "What do you say, Miss Everly? Do you have time for a cupcake?"

She purses her lips, and her dimples pop deep in her cheeks. "How could I possibly say no?" She throws a sarcastic grin over at her mother before bringing her eyes back to mine. "Let me just go grab my dance bag. I'll be right back."

I watch her disappear down a hall, then yank my head back when a delicate hand lands on my arm. "You've met my daughter before, haven't you, Mr. Wilder?"

"I have. We met once over the summer," I admit, a little nervous that she'll ask more.

"She's not the easiest person to get to know, but she has the biggest heart of all my children."

I think about the few conversations Everly and I have had since July and agree with her mom. Definitely not the easiest person to get to know. The big heart is yet to be determined, but I could see it being true. Or maybe, that's just me wanting to see it.

Everly comes back out with sweatpants covering her legs and a bag thrown over her shoulder. She drops a kiss on her mom's cheek. "What time is dinner tonight?"

"Be at the house by six."

Everly nods then looks at Kerrigan, not me. "Are you ready for the best cupcake you've ever had?"

Kerrigan's head bobs up and down, her messy bun smacking me in the face in the process. I drop her down to her feet and take her hand in mine, then follow Everly through the door.

Ten minutes later, we're sitting at a table inside Sweet

Temptations, a bakery I've passed by for years but never been inside before. A hot chocolate with whip cream as big as Kerrigan's head is in front of her, beside one giant chocolate chip cookie and a pink strawberry shortcake cupcake, topped with a chocolate dipped strawberry. Her little eyes are lit up like the Fourth of July as she stares at her mountain of sugar, trying to decide where to start.

When the sugar rush comes crashing down later, there'll be hell to pay, but I'll deal with that when it happens because her smile is everything in this moment.

As if sensing Kerrigan needs help, Everly swipes her finger through her matching strawberry-filled frosting then sucks it between her lips and moans.

Fucking moans . . . And my dick goes from a semi to full-blown hard-on in two point two seconds flat. That one fucking sound is all it takes.

Knowing exactly what she just did, she tosses me a dazzling smile, then gives all her attention to Kerrigan, who's just mimicked Everly's action and now has frosting all over her lips. "Is it good?"

My baby girl's smile is instantaneous as she bobs her head and swipes again before finally picking up the cupcake and biting it. Pink frosting covers her lips, nose, and cheeks, but she loves it right before her strawberry topples to the table.

"She's adorable, Cross."

I drag my eyes back to the goddess sitting across from me. "Thank you."

"I guess I should have asked you some better questions after all." Everly swipes another taste of frosting, and I get the sudden urge to paint that frosting all over her beautiful body.

"Guess so," I agree. "You could ask them now, you know."

Those aquamarine eyes glimmer. "Okay. How about is there a Mrs. Wilder I should know about?"

"There is." I nod and sip my coffee. Damn, this is good.

"You're married?" Everly's eyes bug the hell out of her head like I knew they would.

"No," I shake my head. "Never married. Mrs. Wilder lives in Maine with Mr. Wilder. They were who we visited over the summer. My mom is the *only* Mrs. Wilder. She's pretty amazing too," I add, just to be a dick.

She shakes her head in realization, hiding a relieved smile when it dawns on her that I mean my mom, not my wife. And instead of laughing like I expected, she swipes her finger through the cupcake frosting one more time. Only this time, instead of bringing it to her own mouth, she leans forward and strikes like a snake about to paint my face in frosting.

I catch her wrist in her hand and hold it suspended over the table, then lean forward and watch her beautiful face transform when I suck the frosting off the tip of her finger. A pretty pink flush works its way up her gorgeous golden skin, and a little *oh* slips past her lips before I drop her hand.

The whole thing takes maybe twenty seconds, but time feels like a foreign concept when it comes to Everly. Maybe someday, I'll figure out why.

Her eyes dart to Kerrigan, whose delighted little face is still covered in frosting. She's got the cookie in her hand now and half a cupcake already gone. "Do you like it, little miss?"

My baby girl's eyes go wide again, as if she's surprised Everly's talking to her. Her little head nods up and down, her contented smile growing wider by the moment.

"Stick with me, kid. I can show you all the best sweets in town." Everly sips her coffee, which might as well be a dessert in itself, then turns back to me. "Okay, so no Mrs. Wilder. But what about . . ." She glances at my daughter then back to me. "What about her M-O-M?" she whispers the letters instead of saying the word.

"What about her?" I grind my teeth at the thought of

Helene. "I haven't heard from her since she left months ago. She signed away her rights to . . ." I tip my head toward Kerrigan. "And to Jax," I add.

"Jax?" Everly asks, clearly confused.

"Jax is my baby brother," Kerrigan says without looking up from her hot chocolate.

"Baby brother?" Everly bites down on her lower lip. "Wow. Two kids?"

"Yeah, two kids. And my brother and sister live with me too. I guess you could say I've got my hands full."

I wouldn't blame her if now is when she runs away.

Hell, she probably should get as far away from me as she can.

She's twenty-three. Young and beautiful. The world is in front of her. And here I am, almost a decade older, with two kids and enough baggage to fill her closet full of designer bags. But instead of running, she leans across the table again and runs her finger through the chocolate frosting on the death by chocolate cupcake Kerrigan made me get. "I guess it's a good thing you've got big hands." She slides it between her lips and closes her eyes for a hot fucking second, then opens them and nails me with them. "You still want to take me out, Cross?"

"I told you already, Everly. I'll tell you what I want, and you let me know if that works for you. And what I want hasn't changed." Because I want her.

"I have a one o'clock football game tomorrow. How about you pick me up at six?"

"I can do that."

"Daddy . . . My hands are sticky." Kerrigan holds up her pink frosting-covered fingers, and Everly and I both laugh.

"Yeah, baby girl. They are. Let's go wash up." I stand and scoop Kerrigan out of the chair and catch Everly grabbing her bag from beside her.

"I hope you liked your cupcake, Kerrigan." She smiles as she walks around to my side of the table and pushes a blonde curl away from my baby's face. "I'll see you next week, little miss."

"Bye, Miss Evie," Kerrigan whispers.

"I'll see you tomorrow, Cinderella." Her pretty face pinks up again before she heads for the door.

"Miss Evie looks more like Sleeping Beauty than Cinderella, Daddy."

I turn my face back to my baby as the door shuts behind Everly. "Oh yeah?"

She nods excitedly. "But Miss Evie is prettier," she says with an innocent awe in her voice.

"Yeah, baby. Miss Evie is definitely prettier."

Everly's Secret Thoughts

Sometimes, self-care is reading a book by candlelight in a warm bubble bath. Other times, it's telling someone to fuck all the way off. Depends on the day.

EVERLY

"Are the boys coming tonight?" Grace asks as we round the corner in our parents' gated community. Fall came early to Kroydon Hills, and the sun already sits lower in the dusky sky than it did even a week ago. My parents' neighborhood always looks like it's been ripped right out of a Hallmark movie. Old, tree-lined streets block the views of most mansions, hidden behind perfectly manicured hedges and wrought iron gates. When your dad is the most famous professional quarterback in the country, privacy is something your family values.

And that's before you factor in the rest of our very large family.

My grandfather and uncles have all played professional football or coached the game. Some have done both. Our aunt Sabrina is a congresswoman and former First Daughter. And my cousin Lilah has been singing her way across the country for the past two years on her first big stadium tour, opening up for a famous, former boy bander.

Most of my family lives in this neighborhood these days. Actually, Uncle Brady and Aunt Nattie, and Uncle Murphy and Aunt Sabrina live on the same street as Mom and Dad. But tonight, Mom promised it would just be the eight of us. My parents, my younger brothers—Nixon, Leo, and Hendrix—Grace and me, and our Uncle Tommy.

Uncle Tommy has autism and has lived with Mom since their parents died when he was a little boy and Mom was barely out of high school. He's probably my favorite person in the world . . . Well, next to Grace.

I pull into my parents' long driveway and park my baby-blue Bronco soft-top next to Nixon's truck and watch as my brothers all pile out of it. We like to tease him that it's so big, he's definitely compensating for something else. My youngest brother, Hendrix, hops out of the back of the truck and smacks the hood of my car before I throw open my door and hit him in the stomach on purpose. "Hey, shithead. Watch it."

Leo, three years older than Hendrix and two years younger than Grace and me, smacks Hendrix across the back of the head. "Evil twin will skin you alive if you fuck up her baby."

I cock my head to the side and purse my lips.

He knows me so well.

Grace giggles and throws her arms around our youngest brother. "Hennnnnyyyyyy," she squeals. "You grew."

Hendrix picks her up and squishes her to him. "Two inches since you've been gone. Doc says I've got another one or two in me still."

Nixon rounds the front of the cars and throws an arm around my shoulder. "Told you, little brother. You're a grower not a show-er."

Hendrix grabs his nuts. "How about I show you this?"

"Eww, boys." I gag and shove Nix's arm off me.

The asshole kisses the top of my head, then grabs Grace from Hendrix.

"Helloo . . ." Leo snaps his fingers in front of my face. "What the hell am I? Chopped liver?"

I reach up on my toes and kiss the giant pain in my ass's cheek, then shove him toward Mom and Dad's front door. "Nope. You're my favorite. Just don't tell the others."

Leo and Hendrix both play hockey for Kroydon University. Leo's a junior, and Hendrix is a freshman. They like to act big and bad, but seriously, I'm pretty sure Mom still does their laundry. It's easier to get to see them during the year than Nixon. He's a senior at Boston University, and the Captain of BU's hockey team. Pretty sure he's still a little pissed Dad convinced him to finish his degree instead of entering the draft last year. At least he bitched about it enough last summer.

I follow them all through the front door, and we all make a beeline to the kitchen, where the delicious scent of grilled steak greets us from the backyard. My stomach growls, reminding me I haven't eaten since Sweet Temptations this morning.

"Smells delicious, Momma," Nixon tells Mom before he steals a sliced tomato from a plate covered in tomato salad.

"My babies are all home," she coos and cups his cheek. "This doesn't happen enough anymore."

"I'm just a few hours away, Mom," he tries to argue. But with one look, she shuts him up and makes her way through us all.

"Your father and Tommy are already outside waiting on you. We're eating in the backyard tonight."

The boys head out, and Grace and I stick with Mom.

"Need help with anything?" Grace takes two waters from the fridge and tosses me one, then hops up on the counter until Mom gives her *the eye*, and she hops right back down.

"You could pull the cake I picked up earlier out of the refrigerator so it can come to room temp ." Then she turns

THE WILDCAT

around and a smile curves her lips. "Now you, on the other hand . . ." She points her serrated knife at me. "You need to start talking."

I pick a piece of mozzarella out of the tomato salad and pop it into my mouth. "About what?"

Grace puts a delicious-looking chocolate cake on the counter next to me, then looks between Mom and me. "Ohh . . . What did I miss? What does she need to start talking about?" Grace eyes the cake longingly before deciding to opt for a tomato instead. "Did everything go all right with the baby ballerinas this morning?"

"Everything was fine." I roll my eyes and run a finger through the chocolate frosting. She doesn't know what she's missing. "Damn, that's good."

Grace's shoulders droop. "I wish I had your metabolism."

I slide my finger back to the cake.

"Everly Amelia Sinclair. Do not finger fuck the cake." Grace and I giggle at Mom's use of the F bomb.

"Uh-oh. She cursed *and* middle-named you." Grace's eyes shine. She never gets middle-named because good twin never does anything wrong.

"Yes, I did," Mom agrees, then runs her own finger through the frosting. "Because your namesake, Aunt Amelia, called me after you left Sweet Temptations earlier."

Shit. I should have known she'd do that.

Grace's eyes ping between Mom and me. "Why? What happened at Sweet Temptations?"

Dad walks through the French doors and throws his big arms around Grace and me. "How are my girls doing?"

"Good, Daddy," we answer in unison.

He drops a kiss on Mom's head and grabs a bowl from the counter. "Well, you better come on then. Dinner is ready, and your brothers look hungry."

Mom pushes a second plate into Dad's other hand, then

looks back at me. "We're not done yet, Everly." She picks up the tomato salad and follows Dad outside before Grace smacks me.

"What the hell was that about?"

I grab the pile of linen napkins and take a step back. "Remember the guy I told you about last night?"

Her eyes grow wide with anticipation. "Hot-sex West End guy?"

I nod. Such hot sex.

"Well, turns out his daughter is in your class." I move around her and walk outside, saved by the bell, theoretically.

Or so I thought, until my sister stops at the open door, stunned.

"His daughter," she gasps.

My noisy-ass brothers, uncle, and parents all stop and stare at Grace.

"Whose daughter?" Uncle Tommy asks before sitting down and taking a bottle of beer away from Hendrix. "You're not twenty-one."

Hendrix groans . . . and so do I.

"Damnit, Gracie," I murmur and sit quietly down, taking my place on the other side of Leo.

Grace shrugs and scrunches her nose, then mouths, *Sorry*, before joining us at the table.

"I'm with Tommy." Dad's eye twitches the tiniest bit. "Whose daughter, girls?"

When we don't answer, he looks at the boys. "Do you know anything about this?"

"Don't look at me. I live four hours away," Nix offers as he manages to place a steak on his plate without making eye contact with anyone.

Smart man.

"Oh, good lord. Stop grilling your daughter," Mom groans. "Cross Wilder's daughter. He's a dad at the studio."

"You can question her. Why can't I?" Dad grumbles.

"Cross Wilder, the hockey player?" Hendrix asks around a mouth full of food.

"Chew," Mom chides him while I choke on my water.

"Did you say *hockey player*?" I sputter, gasping for air until Leo smacks my back a little harder than necessary. He pulls out his phone and after a minute, hands it to me.

There he is. All six feet, five inches of tall, dark, and handsome muscle, standing on the ice. His helmet is in one hand, and he's talking to another man, who looks suspiciously like him and also has *Wilder* across the back of his matching hockey jersey.

His *Philadelphia Revolution* hockey jersey.

"Oh, what the fuck?" I mutter.

"Everly," Mom and Dad both snap.

"Sorry. I just—" I cut myself off. Damn it. "I avoid athletes."

At least I try—when I'm not being given the best orgasm of my life by one in a bar.

Damn it.

This is why I don't do strangers.

"What do you mean, you avoid athletes?" Mom counters.

"Let her avoid athletes if she wants to, Belles," Dad snaps at Mom.

"Declan Sinclair," Mom gives it right back to him with a sharp tone. "Your daughters are grown women. They're intelligent. They're beautiful. And thanks to you, they've been raised around overbearing, arrogant, alpha males their whole lives. They're going to date at some point. I wouldn't be surprised if they ended up with overbearing, arrogant, alpha males, also thanks to you. And they're going to demand to be treated well because that's all they've ever seen. Again, thanks to you. You've done your job. Now shut up and let them live their lives the same way you let the boys live theirs."

Dad huffs, refusing to admit Mom is right. "No one will ever be good enough for the girls." Then he looks around the table at the boys. "It's their brothers' jobs to scare the assholes off."

"Again, four hours away," Nixon adds.

"They're not all assholes, Daddy," Gracie tries to placate Dad.

"If they're an athlete, they're an asshole," Nixon agrees, then looks away again. "We're kinda made that way."

Leo and Hendrix mumble their agreement, and Mom's eyes threaten to pop the fuck out of her head like a cat being strangled in a cartoon. I half expect her to hiss at them. "You are not all assholes," she fights back. Yup. There's the hissing. "I raised you better than that."

"Kinda are, Mom." Hendrix shoves a piece of potato in his mouth, then swipes Leo's beer before Grace kicks him under the table, and he begrudgingly gives it back.

"Like I've never had a beer before," he grumbles.

"This is ridiculous. Come on . . ." I argue. "You all know as well as I do, most athletes are oversized alpha males with egos bigger than their muscles and definitely bigger than their brains. They have zero impulse control and shitty tempers. Dad's generation was the last decent one. Now, they're all more interested in their social-media presence and sponsorship deals than they are about being a good guy or treating a woman right. I saw it in college, and I've seen it from the players on the Kings team. The few times I've broken my own rule, I regretted it pretty quickly. And don't even get me started on what happens when you bruise their inflated egos . . ." I bite down on a piece of bread and my tongue before I get myself in the kinda trouble I don't want to bring to my family.

THE WILDCAT

After a few too many silent beats, Mom sighs. "You're too young to be this jaded, Everly."

"If you go on a date with him, you think you can get me his autograph?" Hendrix throws a hopeful plea my way. "He was the Revolution's top scorer last year."

"Your sister isn't going to date a hockey player." Dad sits back in his chair and sips his drink.

"Oh, but it would be fine if she dated a football player, Daddy?" Gracie pokes the damn bear like only the good twin can get away with.

"She's not gonna date him if he's got a kid," Nixon argues.

"Why not?" Grace bites back, and I bury my face in my hands.

Nixon looks at her like she's lost her damn mind. "Because she's not you, Gracie. Evie doesn't do serious. And kids make it serious from the get-go. That's not Evie."

"The hell?" My head snaps up, and I glare at Nixon. "Who says I don't do serious?"

"You do, evil twin," Leo adds.

"She's not evil," Uncle Tommy defends me, then smiles his bighearted, goofy smile. "Maybe a little devious sometimes."

"Hey," I call out, and Uncle Tommy winks.

"I can do serious if I want to. I just haven't wanted too."

I don't bother to tell them I tried once, and it still fucking haunts me.

"Oh my God, I thought that was never going to end." I slam the door of the car and throw it into reverse, ready to get the hell out of Dodge. "Seriously, if I knew my love life was going to be tonight's dinner topic, I would've made you go without me."

"Liar," Grace calls me out. "You'd never say no to Mom and Dad, and you know it."

"Fine. But you know, if you could fuck up at least once in your life, it would really help a sister out." Grace and I have been known as the good twin and evil twin our whole lives. I play along with it most of the time. It's just easier to give people what they expect than to fight to be seen differently.

We've all got our roles to play.

But still . . . it gets old.

"Sorry, Evie. I'll try." *Sure she will.* I think Gracie's world would implode if she ever did anything to ruin her perfect status in our parents' eyes. Not that I fault her for it. In fact, right now might be the first time I envy her instead. "So . . ."

My heart drops a few inches. "So . . . what?"

She turns the music down. "Don't play dumb, Everly. Tell me about *him*."

I drive in silence for a few minutes, trying to choose my next words carefully.

Grace doesn't push for more before I'm ready.

She's the only one in my obnoxiously loud family who won't.

"So . . . I wouldn't hate to get to know him more," I admit hesitantly. "But I'm not sure if that's the smartest thing to do. He's got kids, Grace. *Two kids*. His daughter, Kerrigan, and a baby boy, Jax. I think he's a serious kind of guy."

"So what?" She shakes her head. "Ignore Nixon and Leo. You can do serious if you want to. The question is—do you want to?"

"I don't know . . ." I answer quietly.

I like fun. Fun doesn't hurt.

"Guess you better figure that out." I simultaneously hate that she always knows exactly what to say and love that she'll always call me on my bullshit.

"Yeah . . . I guess so."

THE WILDCAT

*L*ater that night, I'm soaking in a warm bubble bath with my favorite cherry candle lit and my Aunt Nattie's newest romance book up on my kindle when there's a knock at the en suite's door.

"It's Brynlee," Brynn calls through the door.

"Come in," I call back and slip further under the bubbles. Not that we haven't all seen each other naked before, but still... "What's up?"

Brynn sits primly down on the closed toilet seat and fluffs her green-and-white sundress around her legs. "I was just talking to Grace, and she mentioned that West End guy from the summer was Cross Wilder. Why didn't you tell me you hooked up with one of my players?"

"*Umm*... So, I may not have known that little detail until today." Brynn is one of the physical therapists for the Philadelphia Revolution hockey team. I've been so stuck in my own head since dinner, it didn't even cross my mind that she'd know Cross. "We didn't exactly do a ton of talking that night."

Brynn cocks a perfectly shaped strawberry-blonde brow. "He's not exactly your normal type."

"Yeah . . . I figured that out tonight too," I admit sheepishly.

She picks up the towel I threw on the sink before stepping into the deep clawfoot tub, earlier and carefully folds it. "Do you like him?"

"Maybe . . . I don't really know him yet, Brynn. He's a hockey player. Is he even a good guy?"

"He's quiet. Keeps to himself a lot. He's got a brother on the team. Ares. He's the loud one. But Cross . . . well, he's always been nice to me." A shadow crosses her pretty face. "He might be worth giving a chance." She runs her hands over the now-folded white, fluffy towel. "He's not Keith."

My eyes shoot to hers. "I know that."

"Do you? Because I haven't seen you with the same guy twice since that shit happened with him."

"You promised me we wouldn't talk about that," I snap, feeling suddenly vulnerable. And vulnerable isn't a feeling I do well.

"And we haven't," Brynn placates me. "I haven't said a word. I haven't pushed. I haven't told. Not anyone. Even though I still think we should have. Even though I don't think you've dealt with it . . ." she trails off.

When I don't say anything, she places the towel back on the counter and stands. "Cross Wilder doesn't strike me as a guy who's going to play your game your way, Everly. And honestly, I hope he doesn't. I think he could be good for you. But only you can decide to give it a chance."

She turns to walk out of the room, and I want to say something snarky.

To tell her I don't need a guy to be good for me.

I'm fine just the way I am.

But I'm not so sure I believe that anymore.

If I'm being honest with myself, I'm not sure I've been fine for a long damn time.

The Philly Press

KROYDON KRONICLES

WHAT'S IN THE WATER AND WHERE DO I GET SOME?

Holy hotness, Kroydon Hills! Was anyone else lucky enough to be at West End for the mind-blowing reunion that happened last night? The temperature certainly spiked to an all-time high when the newest generation of Sinclair and Beneventi boys–turned–men blew our collective minds. I don't remember the last time we were graced with this many gorgeous guys at one table. What's in the water and where do I get some? In other news, our favorite baller, Callen Sinclair, was there, and surprise, surprise, he went home alone. I guess there's a first time for everything.
#KroydonKronicles #WhatsInTheWater

CROSS

"Where you going, Daddy?" Giant crocodile tears pool in Kerrigan's big blue eyes as she blinks up at me. She looks like I just kicked her imaginary puppy. The one she's been begging for, but I keep saying no. Some days I'm just grateful that I've managed to keep the kids alive for another day. I don't need the responsibility of another living creature. Maybe a fish. They seem low maintenance.

Ares adds a spoonful of peas to Kerrigan's dinner plate, then turns with the fucking devil is in his eyes—the way he always did when we were kids, right before he said something that got me in trouble with Mom. "Yeah, Cross," he drawls. "Where *are* you going?"

I throw my middle finger up behind Kerrigan before I run my hand over her soft hair. "I'm going out with a friend, sweetie. But I won't be long, and I promise to kiss you when I get home."

"You don't have friends," Ares points out like the giant dick he is.

Bellamy hides a laugh next to him as she wipes peach puree from Jax's chubby cheeks.

"Does too, Uncle Ares." Kerrigan's little brows pull together tightly as she frowns up at my brother. "We had cupcakes wif Miss Evie after ballet class yesterday."

Ares slings his arm across the back of Kerrigan's chair and tugs on her curls. "I'm sorry, baby girl. You're right. I was just teasing your daddy." Then the fucker looks at me over her head and grins before giving his attention back to Kerrigan. "How about you tell me more about Miss Evie?"

I grind my teeth and try to remind myself I can't kill him in front of the kids. "Don't grill my daughter for information."

"Aww, come on . . ."

"She's really pretty . . ." Kerrigan answers with wonderment in her voice, her tears long forgotten. "And she knows ballet . . . Oh, oh, and she knows all the best cupcakes."

"Oh, I bet she's got great cupcakes." Ares manages to duck before my hand can connect with the back of his head.

"Watch it," I warn and drop a kiss on Jaxon's sticky cheek. "Thanks for this," I tell my sister. "I won't be too late."

"We're good, Cross. I've got it. Be as late as you want."

Damn. I love my sister. I could have called the nanny tonight, but Bellamy said not to worry about it, and I'd always rather the kids be with family.

One more quick kiss to Kerrigan before I walk out the door and shove the dad guilt down for the night.

Not the easiest thing to do, but for the first time in a long time, I'm looking forward to a night out. I plug Everly's address into the GPS and shoot off a text.

CROSS

On my way.

CINDERELLA

Okay. Text when you're here and I'll meet you in the garage.

CROSS

No.

I'll pick you up at your door.

You may not believe it, but my mother did teach me manners.

CINDERELLA

Never gonna let me live that down, are you?

CROSS

Not planning on it. No.

I'll see you in a few minutes.

Less than ten minutes later, I'm chatting with her doorman.

Yup. Doorman. Because Everly Sinclair lives in *that kind* of building.

The kind with gleaming marble floors, that threaten to blind you when the light hits them just right, and a fancy coffee shop. One that probably charges eight dollars for a cup of black coffee. It's the kind of building where you need to be buzzed in and given a special code for the elevator to go up to her condo.

Once I step into the elevator, I hit the code for the penthouse. Because why wouldn't she live in the penthouse? And who steps on right before the doors close? The bartender from West End, who I'm not entirely sure doesn't have a thing for Everly.

I lift my chin. "Hey, man."

"Still chasing evil twin?" the guy asks while he looks at me like he's assessing a threat.

"Something like that." I cross my arms over my chest and size him up. This guy doesn't intimidate me. I've been playing pro hockey for over a decade. I've gotten into it with bigger, badder guys than this. "You chasing her too?"

I half expect him to throw a punch until he laughs. Hard. "Fuck no. She's psychotic."

Yeah . . . not what I was expecting.

"Dude. No. Seriously. *No*. That one is all yours. If you get stuck for conversation, ask her about the seagulls on the beach. You'll thank me later." The doors open a floor below Everly's, and the bartender salutes me as he shuffles off, mumbling, "Seagulls, man. Trust me."

A minute later, the doors open again, this time on Everly's floor.

Fuck . . . I haven't been on a date in four years, and I feel rusty as shit knocking on her door. Not nervous. But definitely out of my element.

Only it's not Everly who opens the door.

"Hey, Cross. Come on in." Brynlee St. James, one of the team's physical therapists, steps aside, letting me in . . . to a party? "Everly will be out in a minute."

What the fuck?

"Hey, man," my teammate Easton walks over and shakes my hand. "What are you doing here?"

Is this some kind of team party I wasn't told about?

"He's here to pick me up." Everly walks down the hall, and I damn near swallow my tongue. She's gorgeous. A white, fuzzy sweater hangs off one bare shoulder, while her hair hangs down in waves over the other. Tight blue jeans are practically painted on her incredible, shapely legs, and brown boots zip up to her knees. Fuck me . . .

Easton grins like a kid cracked-out on too much sugar. "Oh, this ought to be good."

"Be nice," his wife yells from the couch before moving a blanket away from her chest, exposing her breast and a tiny baby as she switches him to the other side. When I try to avert my eyes, she laughs. "Don't worry. The whole world has seen my boobs lately."

"Princess..." Easton groans.

And a guy I hadn't noticed before covers his eyes as he adjusts an ice pack on his knee. "I don't want to fucking see them. Put that shit away."

"Nobody asked you, Callen," Brynlee snaps back at him as she brings him a bottle of water.

"Come on, Brynn. One beer," he groans, looking at the water like it might as well be piss.

"Suck it, Sinclair. They gave you pain relievers. You don't need beer too." She carefully moves the ice pack and checks his knee before sitting down gingerly next to him. Meanwhile, Madeline Kingston-Hayes, Easton's wife and one of the owners of the damn team I play for, adjusts the baby and turns toward Everly and me.

"So... aren't you going to introduce us, Evie?"

Everly shifts her weight from one long leg to the other, then blows out a quiet breath. "Fine. But you all suck." She points her finger around the room. "And I will get every single one of you back for this." Her voice softens when she peeks down at the baby. "All of you except Griffin."

Everyone in the room laughs at her discomfort, and I'm not sure whether I like it or not. Maybe I'm a bit too overprotective for a first date when I slide my hand to the small of her back and press the slightest bit.

But the smile she throws over her shoulder as she leans into me has me thinking it was a good move.

"Guys, this is Cross."

Everyone in the room says "Hi Cross," like they're Kerrigan's preschool class meeting the new kid.

Everly turns those aqua eyes on me, tonight they're a little more green than blue, and fuck, she's so pretty. "Cross . . . these are my asshole friends. You already know Easton and Brynlee. Not sure about Lindy and Griffin." She points down to Madeline and the baby, then over to the guy with the iced-up knee. "And that dumbass over there is Callen."

"Why am I a dumbass?" Callen pushes back.

"Because you got hurt during the fourth quarter, showing off. Grandpa chewed your ass out in the locker room. And now you're on our couch, sulking like a little baby." She flicks his ear, and he whines like a teenage girl.

Easton leans in next to me. "They take a bit to get used to. But they're not as insane as it looks at first fucking glance."

Everly spins on her heels. "Hmm . . . pretty sure we are, E."

She grabs a small purse off a table, then slips her hand in mine. "Want to get out of here, big man?"

I answer without hesitation, "Yes."

Everly

Cross tugs on my hand, then moves me to the other side of him, so he's the one walking next to the street as we stroll down Main Street later that night. I've seen my dad do the same thing a hundred times, but I've never had a guy do that with me, and I have to roll my lips in to hide my smile. "How did you know that the Fall Festival was one of my favorite things in Kroydon Hills?"

"Lucky guess." He nods toward one of the lines for food, and I shake my head. "So tell me about your friends."

"What do you want to know?" I ask right before I see a

line in front of a stand for my favorite restaurant. "Ohh, Nonna's. Let's go there."

Cross slides his hand from mine and presses it to the small of my back, and I can't decide which I like better. They both give me warm chills.

"You guys seem . . . close."

I look up at him and remember he asked about my friends. I'm learning Cross is a man of few words. I'm not sure I've ever come across that before. I think everyone I know loves to hear themselves talk.

"We are close. You know how you always hear people talk about friends who are more like family? Well, that's us. We were all raised together. Our parents are friends. Brynlee, Lindy, and I all lived together during college. Kenzie, who you didn't meet tonight, and my sister, Gracie, lived with us too. We all stayed together after college and moved into the condo. Lindy moved out when she married Easton last year. Now they're a floor below us. Callen and Maddox live next to them." We move up a bit as the line slowly ambles along. "Next question?" I tease because really, it's me who should be asking him questions. But something about that scares me a little for reasons I'm not 100 percent ready to examine yet.

He shakes his head like he's trying to take it all in. "What's the deal with you and seagulls?"

"What?" I spin around to face him.

Damn, he's handsome, standing in front of me in a long-sleeved green-and-white baseball tee stretched tight over his broad chest and a beat-up old baseball cap pulled down low over his face. He probably thinks he's hiding from prying eyes, but I've seen a few people point as we walk through the crowded street. Kroydon Hills is used to its pro athletes, but there's always one or two people who still get excited. I'd say the interest is another tick against him, but so far, his career seems to be the only tick.

"*Seagulls*. Your friendly neighborhood bartender, who I rode the elevator with earlier, told me to ask you about seagulls." Cross smiles, and my goodness, I think my knees go weak. He's what Grace and I would have called *dreamy* when we were younger. He makes it hard to think straight, and that never happens to me. Boys don't have this effect on me, but Cross Wilder is no boy.

"That fucker," I hiss, silently coming up with plans to retaliate against Maddox. Veering away from seagulls, I point across the street and smile. "See that shop with the purple awning? The one a few down from my mom's dance studio?"

"Nice evasion, Cinderella." He grins and tugs on my hair. "But I'll play along." He runs his fingers along my bare shoulder and up my neck, then leans in close enough for me to feel his warm breath skim my skin. "For now . . ."

Oh holy hell.

"What were you saying, Everly?"

What was I saying? That's a good question.

"That shop," I whisper and point again, this time with a shaky finger. "That's my Aunt Carys's shop. She and her partner, Chloe, design lingerie. I work for them."

"You design lingerie?" Cross pulls back, and his eyes light up with interest as my face flames.

"They've let me design a few things."

"That's impressive." When he says it, I kinda believe him instead of feeling like my dreams are so far out of reach that I'll need a Boeing 747 just to reach them.

"The shop is hosting a fashion show next month. You should come. A few of my friends and I are walking in it."

"Walking? Like modeling the lingerie?"

"Yup," I pop the "p" at the end of the word, then take another step closer to the front of the line. Cross links a finger through a belt loop in my jeans and pulls me back to him.

"As long as I don't have a game that night, I'll be there." The possessiveness in his voice sends a thrill through me before the mention of hockey douses me in ice.

"A game . . . right. *A hockey game.* Your season starts soon." Because he's the one thing I swore I'd steer clear of.

"Our first game is mid-October . . . Maybe you could come. If your friend is Madeline Kingston, I doubt it's the first hockey game you've been to."

"Let's not go getting ahead of ourselves here, big man," I tease. "I've been to a game or two, but football has my heart, and I doubt I'll ever give that away to hockey."

"Fair enough." He flashes a cocky smile. Although Cross would probably call it arrogant. "So you work for your aunt. Teach for your mom. Cheer for the Kings . . . What do you do for yourself?"

"Teaching for my mom was just a favor. Normally, that's Gracie's job. But she's been busy, so I filled in. And I love working with lingerie. But . . ." I blink up at him and lower my voice. "I really want to design wedding gowns. I've been working on my first line for about a year." I'm not sure why I told him that. It's not something I typically share. "I've been saving up for my own shop. But I'm not quite there yet, unless I hit up my trust fund, and I'm trying to do it without touching that."

We move up to the front of the line and place our order for food. Once they hand it to us, Cross carries the plates one block over to the picnic tables set up in front of the park at the center of town and sits down. The late September sun is just dipping down beneath the horizon and bathing us all in a beautiful glow. The lush grass the town mows to within an inch of its life is still a dark green, but the leaves on the trees have started to turn red, ushering in another fall in Kroydon Hills. I love this time of year.

"So tell me about yourself, Cross. I realized yesterday, I

didn't even know you were a dad before I saw you at the studio."

My little white swan who was sitting calmly on my shoulder perks up and runs her hands over her starched tutu. *You didn't know he was a pro hockey player either.*

"Not much to tell. I grew up in Maine. My parents are still there. Left when I was eighteen. Played a few years in the minors. I've been with the Revolution for eight years. Moved to Kroydon Hills after Kerrigan was born. She's three. Jax is about seven months."

"And their mom . . .?" I leave the sentence hanging as I dip a fried ravioli in Nonna's famous marinara sauce and moan around the garlicky goodness.

"She's gone. Decided being a mom wasn't for her. Signed away her rights and left town. Haven't heard a word from her since." He says it with no emotion, as if a mother giving up her children were no big deal.

"Wow. That has to be hard, especially with your long season. The travel schedule alone must suck. It always felt like my dad was gone half the year when we were kids."

Cross's face pales, and I feel like a complete ass.

"We've got a great nanny, and my sister, Bellamy, lives with us. She's a sophomore at Kroydon University and helps when she's not in class. My brother, Ares, lives with us too. But he's on the team with me, so he can't really help most of the time. Besides, some days, I think Jax has a higher emotional IQ than Ares."

"The God of War?" I cock my head to the side and watch Cross's shoulders shake with silent laughter.

"Yeah. It's fitting."

"Sooo . . ." I let my eyes rake over this man and try hard to ignore the memory of his hands on my body. "Is your nanny young and hot?" I dip another ravioli before Cross grabs my wrist and leans across the table. He takes a bite, his lips quickly grazing my fingers, sending shockwaves dancing down my skin. The memory of our first night together crashes over me, ruining any hope I had of trying to forget it.

The weight of his body pressed against me.

His lips. His tongue. His touch.

Yeah . . . that hope goes up in flames.

My black swan jetés over to my white swan, head held high, arms extended out beautifully.

Game on, she announces, thrilled with this new development.

Wanting more. And honestly, who can blame her?

"Well, she's sixty-seven and kind of reminds me of my mom." There goes that smile again. "Soooo, there's that."

"Good answer, Wilder," I whisper.

"I try." Cross pushes the untouched plate of zeppole in front of me once the ravioli is gone.

He watches carefully as I tear a piece off, then pop one of the pillowy bites of heaven into my mouth. I moan around the ball of fried dough dipped in sugar. "You've got to try one of these."

I pick up the remaining piece and hold it up to him, prepared for the zap this time.

At least I thought I was.

But I'm learning quickly, I may never *actually* be ready for Cross Wilder.

He hums deep in his throat. "That *is* good."

I look over his face and drag my thumb through the sugar at the corner of his lips, but Cross has other ideas. He leans across the table and wraps a hand around the back of my neck moments before his lips brush over mine. "But that's even better."

I open my eyes, our faces only a hairsbreadth apart.

Yes. *Yes*, it is.

The Philly Press

KROYDON KRONICLES

PLAYER OR *PLAYER?*

Do we have a NEW COUPLE ALERT, Kroydon Hills? Our favorite blonde bombshell was seen walking hand in hand with the most elusive player on the Philadelphia Revolution. The question is, is he a player or a *player*? Only time and this reporter will tell.
#KroydonKronicles #Blondebombshell #Newcouplealert

EVERLY

There's a knock at my bedroom door later that night before Gracie pads in. Even with her hair thrown up haphazardly on top of her head and an old, baby-pink t-shirt and sleep shorts on, my sister manages to somehow look perfectly put together as she sits down on the bed next to me.

I add a little more detail to the sketch I'm working on before I show it to her and preen when she breathes out a pretty, dreamy sigh. "I love this one, Evie."

"That's because it's white and blush. It's basically half your wardrobe, just fancier."

"I can't help it that my signature colors are blush and bashful."

I add a touch more pink to the sash of the dress. "You always did love *Steel Magnolias*."

"Still do," She tugs a pillow to her lap and runs her fingers through the pink fringe.

Okay, so maybe she's not the only one who likes that color.

"You know she died, right?" We've had this exact conversation a million times throughout our lives.

"Don't remind me." She leans back against my headboard and sighs again. "Are you going to design my wedding dress for me, one day, sissy?"

"Like I'd trust anyone else with that." I link my pinky to hers, then lean my head on her shoulder. "Got the guy picked out yet?"

"Not yet . . . Just the dress. How about you?"

"Hardly," I laugh, trying to sound unaffected.

"Sooo . . . how was your date?"

I close my eyes, and my skin prickles with my memory of Cross's lips on mine. "Awful," I grumble. "But mainly because it was perfect."

"Then why don't you sound happier?" She yanks her finger down, tugging on mine.

"Because I didn't want him to be perfect, Grace. He took me to the Fall Festival."

"The ass," she gasps ridiculously overdramatic. But she's my ride or die to the end.

"You don't understand . . . He opened doors . . . and held my hand." I sit up and toss my sketchbook on my nightstand, then turn toward her and shove my glasses up on my head. "He even walked on the outside."

Grace's eyes double in size. "Like the curbside? Like Dad?"

I nod. "Yup. I've never had a guy do that."

"Nope. Me either," she agrees. *"Rat bastard."*

"What are you doing?" I groan, a little frustrated that she thinks this is funny.

Grace crosses her fuzzy sock-covered feet at the ankle, today's socks are white with bright pink hearts because well, they basically sum up my sister's entire persona perfectly. "I'm trying to agree with you on why your date was awful. I mean, the man had manners. He held your hand, opened doors, and put you on the inside. Something, I might add, Mom swears only the good ones do. Dad says anyone who doesn't is a . . . *pussy* not a man." She whispers the word because as much as Grace doesn't mind cursing, and as far from a prude as she is, crass words still somehow drive her crazy.

"Don't make fun of me," I pout. And yes, I realize I sound like a whiney bitch, and I am legitimately pouting. "I really don't want to like him, and he's making that really hard for me. He's serious. A relationship guy. A dad. And let's not forget, he's a professional hockey player."

Gracie carefully collects the colored pencils that are strewn all over my duvet and places them on the nightstand on her side of the bed, then pulls her knees up against her chest and angles herself toward me. "Break this down for me. I mean, I could totally see a single dad being a serious guy. It makes sense. And if it's the kids that are making you think this might not be for you, you're 100 percent allowed to feel that way." She bends her head so she can see my eyes when I refuse to look at her. "But I don't think that's the real problem."

"We're twenty-three, Gracie . . ."

"We are. And Mom was twenty-three when she was pregnant with us. I'll understand if that's what's really making you pause, but Evie . . . I don't think that's what it is."

I don't say anything because she's right. It's not the kids.

"Did he kiss you goodnight?" Grace continues our stare-off.

I think back to the way he walked me to our door—because of course, Cross wouldn't just drop me off in our garage.

The way his hands cupped my face before his lips lowered to mine.

The chills that skipped along my skin, like electricity skipping along a live wire.

The way I asked him if he wanted to come inside, and the way his answer made me feel.

"No, Cinderella. We rushed this once. Now, we're going to take it slow. You're going to let me take you out again. You're going to let me pick you up at your door, without arguing, and walk you back at the end of the night. Because that's what you deserve, and that's what a man does. We're going to slow this down, so maybe the next time you're acting skittish, you'll stay still instead of pulling away . . . until you're ready to push forward. I'm a patient man, Everly, and something tells me you're worth every second of the wait."

His body crowded mine against the door as he kissed me. Bit down on my lip, then soothed the sting with his tongue until I was aching and needy, and then he was backing away. "See you later, Cinderella."

"Oh wow, seriously?" Grace's cheeks flush, probably matching mine as I tell her about the end of the night.

"Oh yeah." If I close my eyes tight enough, I can still smell him. Sandalwood and soap. All Cross. "Gracie . . . I think I could really fall for this guy."

"I'm going to need you to tell me why that's a bad thing."

"I thought I already did." I tick the reasons off on my fingers. "He's Mr. Serious. A father of two. And a professional hockey player." I hold my fingers up in front of her face. "There's three big, glaring reasons."

Grace laces her fingers with mine and holds our joined hands in her lap. "They sound more like excuses than reasons to me. He's serious. So what? I've seen you be just as serious as anyone I've ever met when you want to be. Don't listen to the boys or anyone else who tries to say you're not. And boo-freaking-hoo, he's an athlete. So was Dad, and Uncle Brady, Uncle Murphy, and Uncle Bash. Not to mention Grandpa. Our brothers are athletes. Callen's an athlete."

"Callen may not be your strongest example here," I interrupt.

"True. Okay, manwhore aside . . ." She bites down on her lip and hides her smile. "Ignore Callen. But seriously. Dad worships Mom. And you can't tell me our uncles don't worship our aunts. Uncle Brady and Aunt Nattie are what half her books are based on. There's a whole TV show about them, and they got together in high school. I get what you were saying yesterday about athletes. But . . . what if Cross is the exception to that rule and you miss out because you lumped him in with the jerks you've dated before?"

"Grace . . ." I plead, but I'm not really sure what I want to hear her say.

"You'll never know if you don't give him a chance."

"But he'll never hurt me without that chance either," I counter quietly. So quietly that if it weren't Gracie sitting across from me—Gracie, who I swear I have *twintuition* with—no one else would ever hear the barely whispered words. But Gracie and I understand each other on a different level. We always have.

"We all get hurt at some point, Evie. That's why the good things in life feel so good. If everything was easy, how would anything be amazing?"

"I hate that you're always right," I admit, exasperated. "This is why you're the good twin."

"No. They call me the good twin because you scare them. You're the fearless twin. You always have been. You try everything first, so when I do something, it's easy because I already know it's safe. It's been like that since we were little. And when I didn't like to talk, you did it for me. They said you were loud, but you weren't. You were protective. It makes you seem wild and bossy and makes me seem sweet and shy. When in reality, you were brave, and I was scared." She tucks her feet under my blanket and turns off the light next to her. "Can I sleep here tonight, sissy?"

I hit the switch on the light next to me and pull the blanket up over us. "Always, Gracie."

"Did you finish your design for the finale yet, Everly?" Aunt Carys looks over my shoulder at the gown I'm sketching behind the register at Le Désir, and I flip back to the previous page to show her my design for the fall fashion show.

"Put the finishing touches on it this morning. I just want to find the right lace." I run my finger over the swatches I've got sitting next to me. "Neither of these are right."

Carys let me design the panties Gracie and I are both wearing. She and Chloe designed the rest.

"I still can't believe you got the Kingstons to agree to this," Carys adds as she looks at the lace options again.

"My best friend is one of them. Once I had her on board, it didn't take too much convincing. None of them can say no to Lindy." When I came up with this idea a few months ago, I figured it was a long shot. Carys and Chloe's lingerie is so delicate and sexy, but they wanted to branch out in their marketing. My idea was sporty. This town, and half of the high-end clientele from the city who shop here, have some kind of tie to professional sports. So my friends and I are going to walk the runway in the finale in the most expensive lace and silk panties. Boy cut, bikini, French cut, hipster, and a thong. But with a local sports twist.

I'm still shocked Brynlee agreed to the thong. But she really has a great ass, so who can blame her? Brynn works out daily at Crucible, her dad's MMA gym. That girl squats like her life depends on it, and her body is insane.

"And you're sure your dad is okay with this?" Carys pushes. She's asked this multiple times, and I keep giving her the same answer. You'd think by now, she'd stop asking.

"I'm twenty-three. I don't need Dad's permission to walk a runway if I want to."

Carys is Dad's stepsister, and she's married to Dad's younger brother, Cooper. But that's a whole other story . . . Her mom married Grandpa after Uncle Cooper graduated and joined the Navy. That's why, even though Callen is only a week older than Grace and me, he's our uncle. Definitely an oopsie baby. And we never let him forget it.

Carys glares at me with eyes the same color as Callen's. They turn a darker shade of green when either of them is mad, and hers are shining like the darkest emerald I've seen in a long time at the moment. "You might be old enough to vote and drink, kiddo, but I'm still young enough for your father to kill me."

"Mom won't let him." I close my sketchbook and place it under the counter when Maddox's little sister, Caitlin, and another girl walk into the shop. "Hey, Kit Cat."

Carys nods toward the back of the store, where she keeps an office, then walks away.

"Hey." Caitlin runs her hand along a sheer black-and-white polka-dot babydoll set hanging in the front of the store as her friend stays quietly at her side.

"You're going to get me killed if you buy that, kid," I warn.

"Everly . . ." she pouts, and her friend's head snaps up.

"Don't *Everly* me. I'm not saying I won't sell it to you, I'm just saying don't mention my name if your mom sees it."

"Don't you mean my dad?" Cait asks.

"Hell no," I laugh. "The entire city might fear your dad, but Aunt Amelia scares the shit out of me. Uncle Sam freezes the second we say *girl problems*. Did you see him when I asked if your mom had a tampon after dinner last month? I thought he was going to die."

She laughs, but her friend is still staring, so I walk over and introduce myself. "Hi. I'm Everly. Can I help you find something?"

The young woman with long, dark hair and tiny, delicate features, looks up at me, unsure. "Umm. You have a pretty name." She smiles and adds, "It's unusual."

"Thank you," I answer, a little caught off guard.

"I'm Bellamy," she says hesitantly. "Wilder."

Well shit.

I'm soaking in the tub when my phone rings later that night, and not gonna lie, I'm more than a little surprised to see Cross's name flash across the screen. "Hey, big man," I answer as the FaceTime connects.

Oh my . . . Cross is lying down on what I guess is a hammock outside, judging by the dusky sunlight and the gentle sway of the phone. A chubby ball of baby is tucked under his chin, wrapped in a red, navy-blue muslin blanket. I can't quite explain the way my heart sinks over the exquisite sight.

"Hey, Cinderella," his tired voice drawls.

"Who do you have there?" I ask as I balance the phone, making sure he's only seeing my face instead of a bubble-bath peep show.

"Are you in a bathtub, Everly?" His lips tip up in a sexy smile that makes me wonder if my vibrator is waterproof.

"Maybe. Are you on a swing? The phone is moving."

"Jax is teething, and it's making the little man miserable

tonight. The movement of the hammock always knocks him right out. Pretty sure I'm gonna end up sleeping out here one of these nights." He presses his lips to the fine hair on Jax's head. "How are you doing? How was work and practice?"

"Practice was easy. The team's away this weekend, so it's a lighter week. Work was . . ." I think about my surprise customer. "Well it was a little more interesting."

"Oh yeah?" There's something about his voice tonight.

He sounds tired.

Why does tired sound sexy?

My white swan yawns, stretching her arms above her head. *Because he's tired from taking care of his family. It doesn't get sexier than a man taking care of the people he loves.*

My black swan rolls her eyes before she leaps away. *Orgasms are sexier.*

But right now, I'm not thinking about orgasms.

Right now, all I'm thinking about is how much I'd like to be lying in his arms too.

Fuck my life.

"Everly . . ." Cross verbally nudges me.

Oops. "I met your sister today."

"Really?" He smiles before his brows furrow and wrinkle. "What the hell was she doing in the shop?"

"Most women buy lingerie in a lingerie shop, Cross," I tease quietly.

"Women buy lingerie for their man to see. Bellamy doesn't have a man . . . or a woman." His smile vanishes from his face.

Now it's my turn to smile. "Women buy lingerie to feel beautiful for themselves. Not a man. Not a partner. I mean, it's nice when someone else can appreciate it, but you've got to be able to appreciate it for yourself first."

"Have I told you how incredibly sexy I find your confidence, Everly?" he growls, and I feel the bass in his voice from the very tip of my toes all the way to the top of my head, and it feels divine.

"No . . . you haven't mentioned that." I don't tell him how much I like that he did.

"It's incredibly attractive. It's the first thing I noticed that night in West End. I was listening to the way you were talking to the bartender—"

"Maddox," I interrupt.

"Yeah, him. I hadn't turned to look at you. I was just listening to you spar with him. You exuded confident woman. You didn't take his shit—"

"He wasn't really giving me shit, Cross," I push back.

"Would you stop interrupting me?" he teases as his voice lazily caresses my warm skin. "This is my memory. And I remember you handing him his ass and thinking, *Damn . . . I need to know that woman.*"

"Oh yeah . . . Well, I guess you got to know me."

"Pretty sure I didn't even crack the outer shell yet."

Jaxon's tiny, balled-up fist breaks free from the blanket, and he lets out a miserable cry.

"I'll talk to you later, big man."

"Night, Cinderella."

Our call ends, and I drop my phone on the counter, then submerge myself under water, hoping to drown out the noise in my head. Because right now, I'm pretty sure it would be all too easy to fall hard and fast. And I'm not sure I can let myself do that. Not again. Not even for him.

The Philly Press

KROYDON KRONICLES

HELLO PUCK PACK

The fifties had the rat pack.
The eighties had the brat pack.
Does our decade have the *Puck Pack*?
Boone Kent, Ares Wilder, AJ Benson, and Nash Whitters have been spotted out on the town multiple times over the past few weeks. However, last night, they were photographed indulging in good times, good booze, and good-looking friends . . . Friends made up mainly of the, shall we say, *fairer sex*. One such *friend* managed to snap quite the revealing selfie with a very unclothed Mr. Benson and Mr. Whitters in compromising and slightly uncomfortable-looking positions with herself and one other lucky lady. Rumor has it the Philadelphia Revolution management is less than thrilled. Apparently, not all press is good press. Stay tuned for an update, all you beautiful people.
#KroydonKronicles #PuckPack

CROSS

There's a reason why I never let myself get out of shape in the offseason . . . And practices like today are the prime fucking example of why. More than one guy puked up last night's booze after Coach handed us our asses for hours. Suicides, sprints, and working the damn boards the whole fucking practice, while he bitched about the stupidity of the *Puck Pack,* pretty much equaled a dumpster-fire practice.

Can't say I blame Coach for being pissed.

It only takes one or two guys to fuck it up for everyone.

And holy shit, did they fuck it up last night.

By the end of practice, I'm sore as shit and slow as hell. It doesn't help that I was already fucking exhausted because Jax's gone on a damn sleep strike this week. If he's sleeping on me, he's perfectly content. The minute I try to put him in his crib, he wakes up screaming. So no, I'm not in the mood to be lectured more once Coach has had his say. Especially not when our team captain, Jace Kingston, decides he wants to tear the whole team a new asshole too.

"We're a team. If one of us goes down, we all go down.

Got it?" His angry voice booms through the locker room just before Boone laughs out loud, saying something about Whitters going down.

Holy fuck. Kingston loses his fucking mind.

Yeah. I'm out.

That's when I leave the shitshow and head to the showers.

I'll deal with Ares when I get home tonight.

At least he wasn't in the damn pictures.

Would have been better if he wasn't involved at all.

I let the hot water beat down on me, soothing my sore muscles before I make my way back to my locker and find Jace waiting for me. At least he looks slightly less pissed than he did a few minutes ago. "You okay, Cap?"

"Fucking idiots," he groans.

I'm half expecting him to tear into me about keeping a better eye on my brother, but he grabs something from his pocket instead and tosses it to me. "Thought you might want to have this since our first preseason game is next week."

I look down at the white capital A on a navy-blue patch. *Well shit.* I run my thumb over the white stitching and swallow down the emotions that come with this.

In our league, there aren't captains and assistants.

You're allowed one captain and up to three *alternates*.

Some teams chose three, others have one.

The my time with the Revolution we've had two.

If you want to get technical, a captain is the only player on the ice who can officially question a ref about a call during a game. If he's on the bench, an alternate can take his place on the ice.

But unofficially, captains and alternates are the leaders of the team. On and off the ice. They set the tone of the team. Some say the season. They're the guys you want the rookies and new guys to look up to. The guys who can speak for the team in front of the camera and behind closed doors.

THE WILDCAT

The last few years, Kingston has been our captain, with Boone and Jonesy as our alternates. But Jonesy retired after our playoff run last season, and rumor has it, Kingston might be following him out at the end of this season.

"Seriously, man?" I ask him, fucking shook.

I work hard. I'll never give anyone a reason to question that. But when I'm done, I don't mentor the younger guys. I go home to my family. I don't talk to the press. I keep my head down. I don't hype everyone up in the locker room. I leave that to guys like Kingston and Boone. The ones who like to be loud.

I do my thing but never needed everyone looking at me to do it.

"You deserve it, Wilder. If you're gonna take my patch when I retire, I'm gonna need you to start getting your feet wet now." Kingston's a fucking legend. He's been playing for this team for close to two decades. He's got twelve cups under his belt. *Twelve.* We became one of the consistently best teams in the league on his back.

I close my hand around the white-stitched patch. "What about Boone?"

"Boone's a great alternate, but he doesn't want the C. He's too hotheaded. Kinda like that brother of yours." The look he gives leaves no doubt exactly what he thinks of the shit Ares, Boone, and the others were involved in last night, same as I do. "They're both great to have in your corner, but not who you want talking to the press. That was Jonesy's job. And now it's yours."

"Yeah, I get that. So the retirement talk is serious then?"

"I've talked with Coach. It's not a done deal yet. But I've been promising my wife I'd consider it more seriously this year. She likes to tell me I'm getting old." He shrugs. "Wish she was wrong, but my body is telling me otherwise. That surgery after the playoffs last year would have been nothing to recover from even five years ago. This time, it took me the whole damn offseason. Not sure I've got another one of those in me."

"Seriously, I'm honored, Cap."

"You're going to need to work harder than you ever have, Wilder." He leans back against my locker, and I have this feeling I'm about to get the compliment in a shit sandwich.

"I need you bonding with the guys. They all respect your game, but the team needs more. Especially now. We need you to build those relationships. When it's your turn to set the tone in this locker room, you need their buy-in. Trust me. It makes everything easier. You're a silent motherfucker with a killer work ethic. We're gonna need you to put yourself out there more. With the guys. With the press."

"Yeah . . . I get it," I grumble. "Doesn't mean I like the sound of it though. I fucking hate the dog and pony show. I'm not the guy who's ever gonna want to sit down for the post-game press."

"Well, you better get used to it." He picks up the folded jerseys I hadn't noticed sitting in my locker before now. "Now get moving so I can make the announcement to the guys. I need to get home in time for my daughter's soccer game."

Alternate captain.

Well, I'll be damned.

I decide to swing by Sweet Temptations on my way home and grab cupcakes for Kerrigan and Bellamy and order a coffee for Everly while I'm there. According to that woman, she runs on caffeine, and I'm pretty sure she still at Le Désir .

An older woman behind the register smiles when she hands me the coffee. "That's a very specific coffee order, Mr. Wilder."

Damn small town. Everyone knows your name. "It's for a very specific girl . . . if she's still at work."

"She's still there." Her smile grows. "Have a nice night."

Small. Fucking. Town.

The bells above the door in the lingerie shop chime when I walk in, and a petite brunette looks up from a rack of sheer bras. "Hi. Welcome to Le Désir. Can I help you find something today?"

"Uh . . . I was hoping to find Everly," I half mumble, caught off guard for the second time in just a few minutes.

The woman by the rack hides her laughter at my obvious discomfort. "Can't say I have one of those for sale."

"Hey, Aunt Carys . . ." Everly walks out from a back room, holding up two pairs of red lacy panties with thick satin ribbons. I'd like to see them on her, just so I can untie them with my teeth.

I angle my body behind a rack of robes, so they don't see the effect the sight of this woman has on me.

"There's someone here to see you, Everly," the tiny brunette whispers something else I can't hear, then takes the panties away from a frozen Everly. "I'm going to put these away. You can get out of here if you want. I'll close up."

She moves past Everly, who finally shakes off her surprise and blinks up at me with her beautiful eyes. "Thanks, Aunt Carys . . ." her voice trails off, and she runs her palms over her short black skirt, straightening it. "What are you doing here, Cross?"

I hold up the cup of coffee. "I stopped by Sweet Temptations on my way home and thought you might like a cup of coffee."

"Thanks." She steps forward, her long lashes fluttering

behind black-rimmed glasses. That—combined with the black skirt, white blouse, black catholic-schoolgirl heels, and a black velvet bow holding up half her hair—has my cock so fucking hard, you could use it as a goddamned hockey stick.

"Come over to my house for dinner." The words are out of my mouth before I even realize what I'm saying. I don't bring people home. Not women. Not friends. Not anyone. My house. My family. My kids. They're private.

"Tonight?" It sounds so innocent. "Like a second date?" She's hesitant—like a deer caught in headlights.

"No . . . Not a date." I run a hand over her hair and tug. "Just have dinner with me."

My skittish girl chews her bottom lip as she contemplates my offer. "What about your kids?"

I tilt her head up to my face. "What about them?"

"What are they going to think?"

"Pretty sure Jax is going to cry because that's all he's done all week, and Kerrigan may try to get you to put on a tutu. She's barely taken hers off. Not that I'd complain about seeing you in a tutu, Cinderella. Just saying . . . Anything past that, I'm not sure my kids will even care."

She sighs, soft and sweet. "A tutu, huh? I could probably make that happen, you know."

I wrap my arm around her waist and press closer. "I'll save that for another day. I'm going to be dreaming about this sexy librarian way you look right now for fucking days."

Everly licks her glossy pink lips, and my cock jumps in my pants. "Oh yeah?"

"Yeah," I groan as my lips graze hers on their way to her ear. "Say yes, Everly."

"Not a date."

"Dates are romantic. Trust me, a screaming baby and the Disney channel are about as far away from romance as you can get." Hopefully, it's not as bad as it sounds, but I'm probably setting us up for a shitshow.

Everly

My pulse races as I call my sister from the Bluetooth in my car while I follow Cross to his house.

Thankfully, my sister picks up after the first ring. "Hey," she answers, breathing heavy. "I've got five minutes before I have to be back in the studio. What's up?"

"Holy shit, Grace. He walked in the shop in gray sweatpants and a white t-shirt, and his hair was wet, and his ball cap was on backward, and . . . *and* he remembered my coffee order and brought me exactly what I like, and now I'm on my way to his house to have dinner with him and his kids, and I'm freaking the fuck out a little bit here."

"He brought you coffee?"

"One pump chocolate, one pump raspberry."

"Holy shit. That's like your love language," she squeaks.

"I. Know."

"Okay, breath. You can do this. Pull your big panties up and act like the bad-ass bitch you are."

"A, my panties are not big." A ridiculously loud snort rips from her throat, but I ignore it. "And B, was that your idea of a pep talk?"

"Listen. I'm starving. I'm sore. And I'm horny. And you're bitching because a gorgeous man in gray sweatpants, that probably show off what I'm betting is an enormous dick, brought you coffee and is taking you home to make you dinner. Bad-ass bitch is better than calling you a scaredy cat.

Now, embrace the fear. Enjoy the dinner. And let him get to second base. Love you. Gotta go." She makes a kissing sound into the phone before disconnecting the call, and I screech into my empty car.

Not helpful, Gracie.

So much for sisterly solidarity.

Cross turns into Lindy's old neighborhood on Kroydon Lake, and I follow him to the far end of the neighborhood with the older, bigger properties, that back up to the biggest part of the lake and falls. We pull down a driveway that's got to be nearly half a mile long, lined with old oak trees and covered in burnt orange leaves on either side of the lane. The driveway stops next to a restored farmhouse that looks like something you find on an episode of HGTV after a contractor spent a fortune bringing a gorgeous old house back to its original glory. Flower baskets hang from a white porch that looks like it wraps 360 degrees around the entire house. It's beautiful.

I grab my bag from the front seat and walk over to Cross's truck, trying to ignore the nerves clawing at me.

He's got a Sweet Temptations bag in one hand and a hockey bag thrown over his shoulder. And my goodness . . . He really does makes sweatpants look almost pornographic, and I'm here for it.

He looks at me, like he's expecting me to bolt at any moment, and guilt mixes in with my nerves. "You ready for this?"

I have a split-second to decide Gracie's right. I'm a bad-ass bitch, albeit with tiny, sexy, panties. I decide what I want to do. And I decide what I'm comfortable with. I straighten my shoulders and pull up my proverbial panties. I can do this. "Sure. Kids love me."

Cross presses his palm to my back—the way I'm learning he likes to do . . . and I'm starting to enjoy—and guides me to the side door of the house. "The kids are easy. It's my brother who's probably gonna be a pain in the ass."

"Oh, pain-in-the-ass brothers, I can handle."

We walk into the house, and Cross dumps his hockey bag in a white-paneled mudroom, lined with cubbies for coats and shoes. A sparkly purple backpack sits neatly in one, while a black minty green Macbook charges in the one next to it. And I'm reminded that I've been invited into his personal space, and I don't get the feeling that's something Cross takes lightly.

We move into a country chic kitchen and Cross drops the Sweet Temptations bag on the counter before a slightly younger-looking version of him pops up from where his face is stuffed in the fridge. "Hey, asshat. Did you bring home din . . . ner?"

He looks at me, dragging his eyes over me from the bow in my hair down to the toes of my shoes, and I resist the urge to flinch. Instead, I lift my eyes to Cross. "You Wilder boys do not make the best first impressions, do you?"

"Yeah . . . That's Ares," Cross groans. "Watch out for him. He's not housebroken."

"Dude. I'm not a fucking dog," Ares argues as Bellamy walks in, holding a cranky-looking baby, who I'm assuming is Jax.

"You're totally a dog, and nowhere near housebroken. You're also kinda always in heat." She hands Jax off to Cross. "Don't bother denying it just because Everly is here."

"The fuck? I'm not in heat." He pulls a bottle of vitamin water from the fridge and glares at his sister. "How do you know who she is?" Ares asks, and I realize he kind of reminds me of Leo. "And why's everyone picking on me?"

"Because you just checked me out like I'm a stripper," I tell him, and Cross and Bellamy both turn and stare. "What?" I ask Cross. "I told you I can handle brothers. I've got three of them."

"I'll let you handle me any time you want, blondie." Ares smiles, and Cross growls. Legit growls. And it's surprisingly hot. Like panty-melting. And I'm wearing expensive panties.

"Choose your next words very carefully," Cross warns Ares, and the bass in his tone does warm, tingly things to my body.

Down girl, my little white swan shushes me. You're in a room full of people.

Ares pops a goofy grin. "You're no fun today, Criss Cross."

"Maybe because Coach worked all our asses off just to punish you guys for acting like fucking douchebags last night." Cross moves over to the fridge and takes a teething toy out of the freezer.

Jax's chubby little hands grab for it immediately before his daddy rubs it over his gums.

Holy hot daddy. Why is Cross with a baby in his arms unbelievably sexy?

Like my body temp is heating up—hot.

"Coach was overreacting," Ares bitches, and I laugh.

That's when both brothers turn to stare at me.

Oops.

"Sounds like your coach is trying to get the team to get its own teammates in check," I note. Sports, I can talk about. I've been surrounded by athletes my entire life. This is strangely my comfort zone. And yes, I hear the ironic way that sounds, considering athletes are the definition of what makes me uncomfortable.

Christ . . . Now I might as well be having a full-blown two-way conversation with myself.

"What would you know about it, blondie?" Ares questions, clearly not liking my truth bomb.

"More than you, apparently," I snap back. "One coach

yelling at you is only so effective. Pissing off an entire team, so they all start policing you, is much more efficient."

"What are you, a hockey savant?" Ares grumbles.

"Nope. Football is more my sport."

"Miss Evie?" a little voice asks before I see Kerrigan in the doorway in her dance skirt. She walks to Cross and wraps an arm around his leg.

"Hey, sweet girl," he bends down and kisses his daughter, and the first little piece of the heavily fortified wall around my heart cracks. The way this man is with his kids is incredibly attractive.

"Miss Evie is going to have dinner with us tonight. Is that okay?" he asks her.

Kerrigan looks from her father to me, then nods her small head.

I carefully squat down to her level, making sure my skirt doesn't rise too far up my legs in the process. "Hey, Kerrigan. Have you been practicing?"

She nods again. "Every day," she answers quietly. "I'm watching *Rapunzel*. Want to watch wif me?" She offers me her hand, and I glance at Cross quickly to make sure this is okay.

Only he's not looking at me.

His eyes are locked completely on his daughter.

Something between shock and awe shining back.

After a minute, he tears his dark eyes from her, and I think the ground shifts beneath my feet from the pure emotion coming off him in waves.

This man isn't a player. It's written on every cell of his DNA.

It's in the way he looks at his daughter and the way he holds his son.

The way he brought me home to meet his family after one date.

Still doesn't mean I'm not scared of giving him the power to hurt me.

But maybe . . . *maybe* I need to try and take a few baby steps.

With his okay, I wrap my hand around hers. "Lead the way, kiddo."

Her little body vibrates with excitement as she starts to chatter. "Aunty Bellamy and me were watching Rapunzel. I like her better than Cinderella. Her prince is Flynn Ryder. He's the bestest."

I look over my shoulder at Cross and mouth, *Told you so*.

"He sure is, kiddo."

CROSS

"Well, she's a smoke show and a ball buster." Ares watches Kerrigan lead Everly out of the kitchen. "Any chance she's got a sister?"

"She's got a twin sister," I tell him, only partially paying attention as I move across the kitchen so I can see my girls sitting down together on the couch. Because whether that woman in the other room knows it yet, she's my girl.

Ares whistles. "Seriously?"

"She's got three brothers too. She's a Sinclair," Bellamy tells him as I sway with Jax in my arms, enjoying the way my quiet, shy daughter is talking to Everly like they're old friends. She's not whispering. She's smiling like it's Christmas morning and Everly's her very own doll.

"What's a Sinclair?" My brother asks, completely confused, and Everly giggles from the couch, then catches my eye from across the room and smiles the most beautiful smile. Guess she can hear us.

Bellamy groans in frustration. "Her dad is Declan Sinclair, and her grandfather is the Kings coach."

"How the fuck do you know that?" Ares bitches.

"Because Caitlin's family and her family are good friends." That gets my attention.

"What?" I turn and look at my sister. "Really? Your friend from school?"

"Yeah. Cait's mom owns Sweet Temptations, and she's best friends with Everly's mom."

Now the woman smiling at me when I ordered the coffee makes sense.

"They're all basically Kroydon Hills royalty. Do you even pay attention? Cait's brother, Maddox, owns West End, and she says he and Everly live in the same building," Bellamy adds, and another piece of the puzzle falls into place.

"The bartender," I groan.

"Yeah," Bellamy takes a pan of lasagna out of the fridge and pops it in the oven. "They're all friends."

"Dude. She's hot, and she knows sports. You better lock that shit down."

Jax waves his teether around and accidentally smacks Ares in the face while I laugh. "You know you're a douche, right?"

The fucker smiles. "It's one of my better qualities."

"I'll just let you keep thinking that."

One burned lasagna, a spilled jar of apples, and a very long toddler meltdown at bedtime later, and I finally walk quietly downstairs with the baby monitor in my hand to find Cinderella wiping down the counter in a quiet kitchen. She lost her heels at some point during the night, and after an unfortunate encounter with a less than enthusiastic Jax and a jar of corn that splattered all over her white blouse, one of my t-shirts is now hanging off her gorgeous body, covering her skirt, stopping mid-thigh.

She's fucking gorgeous.

I move in behind her and grip the counter, bracing my hands on either side of her body, and Everly sucks in a breath. "What are you doing, Cinderella?" I run my lips over her ear and enjoy the way she shivers in my arms. "There's no evil stepmother here. You don't have to clean."

Everly drops the rag to the counter and leans her head back against my shoulder. "I don't know . . . I'm wearing rags," she murmurs back with a low, sexy, teasing tone to her sultry voice.

"Hey, it's loved, not rags." I slide my hands to her hips, then spin her around and boost her up to sit on the counter. Her gorgeous eyes grow wide. They're more turquoise now with flecks of green dotting her irises. "I'll have you know that the Wildcats were my high-school hockey team, and we were the Main State Champs three years in a row."

"Oh yeah?" She wraps her arms around my neck and runs her fingers through my hair. "You were a Wildcat?" One blonde brow arches, and a dimple pops deep in her cheek.

"Fuck. You're so pretty." I let my hand move up her back until I'm cupping her head. "Thanks for coming to dinner."

Her pupils darken as her hand snakes up the front of my shirt. "Cross . . . I don't do this."

"Don't do what?" I ask, somehow knowing her answer could change *everything.*

She's quiet while her eyes beg me to understand.

"I don't date. I don't do relationships." She slides her hands up my chest before digging her fingers in the hair at the nape of my neck. "I don't do this."

"But you came . . ."

Her expressive eyes hold mine for a second, followed by the tiniest nod. "You're a hard man to resist."

"Then don't." I twirl a lock of her hair around my finger. It's silky soft, and I want to feel it dusting my skin when she throws her head back, screaming my name.

Her eyes keep focusing on my lips, and it takes every ounce of strength I have to not slam my mouth against hers and take what I want.

"I need us to take this slow, Cross." She ghosts her lips against mine.

"Your pace, Everly. My life gets crazy when the season kicks into full gear, and it's a long fucking season. But I'm here, and I know what I want."

"You're going to destroy me, Cross Wilder."

"I'm pretty sure you're going to save me, baby." I drag her to the edge of the counter, my fingers digging into the globes of her ass, taking my time. She's okay with rushed, but this woman needs to know she deserves so much more than that. I brush my lips over hers, and that cherry taste that is so completely Everly explodes on my lips.

Her long legs lock around my waist, and she whimpers as electricity sparks between us and thunder booms in the distance.

I hear my brother's heavy feet hitting the stairs and pick Everly up.

"Where—"

I press my lips to hers and grab the monitor from the counter. "Shh, Cinderella."

A few steps later and I've got her outside. I sit us down on the oversized lounge chair in the dark corner of the wrap-around porch as the first drops of rain hit the lake in the distance. "I'm done sharing you tonight."

She straddles my lap, and her skirt inches up to her hips. My hands follow the same path.

"I love the rain," she whispers, looking out at the lake. "It's so pretty."

"Yeah," I agree, never taking my eyes from her. "Beautiful."

Everly turns back to me and drags her finger along my lip. "What am I going to do with you, Cross?"

"Anything you want." And I mean every word of it. I trail my mouth along her jaw as the humidity clings to us like a second skin. One I want gone. But I promised we'd take this slow.

Everly wiggles in my lap, trying to get closer. To quench the need. Her chest rubs against mine. Soft curves fit perfectly against hard planes, just like I knew we would.

Our tongues dance a torturously slow dance. Like it's our first kiss. Learning. Reconnecting. Setting every fucking nerve-ending aflame while the lightning cracks above the lake, illuminating her gorgeous face for seconds at a time.

Long enough to see the want.

The need.

Long enough to know I'm not in this alone.

The wind whips warm drops of rain under the darkened safety of the porch, dampening our skin. I run my tongue down her neck, licking every last drop, stopping to trace lazy circles over her racing pulse.

Everly clings to me as we make out like two teenagers in the dark, until the crackle of the monitor, followed by Jax's piercing cry, stops us.

She pulls back first and drops her forehead to mine.

We're both breathing heavily as I wait to see if Jax will stop crying.

"I should probably get going."

I press my lips to her forehead. "You gonna run, Cinderella?"

"Not yet, big man."

It's the *yet* that I've got to work on.

Everly's Secret Thoughts

You don't have to marry the prettiest girl at the game. Marry the girl screaming the loudest because her team is losing. That girl is going to raise winners, and you want your kids to be winners.

EVERLY

I drop down onto our couch Sunday afternoon, cradling a bowl of popcorn and my sketchbook, as we all pile on to watch the Kings hopefully destroy Dallas. I hate away games. There's nothing like being in the stadium. The energy. The intensity. I freaking love it.

I wish the cheerleaders traveled with the team, but we only cheer at home games. Our team typically makes the playoffs, though, so we do travel for those games. Same for the championship, when we make it to those, which luckily, we've done a few times during my time cheering for the team.

"So, Evie . . ." Brynn throws a piece of popcorn at my face to get my attention. "What's going on with Cross?"

"Oh, come on. We're watching football. Don't pull the girl-talk shit during the game," Maddox grunts, then ducks when Brynn tosses a pillow his way so it hits Kenzie instead.

"Hey!" Kenz turns around and smacks him with it. "Do not make me an innocent bystander."

"Like you're so innocent." Maddox clenches his jaw, like he doesn't secretly love us all. "Yell at Brynn, not me."

"It's not like the game has started yet." I grab the bowl of popcorn from Brynn and stuff a handful in my mouth.

"Take your time and chew. I can wait you out, evil twin," she threatens, and I know she will. I've been avoiding talking about Cross since I came home in his shirt last week. Of course, all the girls were home and in the kitchen when I walked in the door and refused to talk about it. "You're smiling, Everly."

"Nothing's going on. We're talking."

Kenzie looks up from whatever med school assignment she's got her nose buried in. "When are you seeing him again?"

I flip open my sketchbook and grab my pencil. "I'm not sure."

"Why don't you invite him over to watch the game today?" Brynn asks, her voice saccharine sweet as she steals back the popcorn.

"It starts in thirty minutes. I'm not asking him now. I'll look like an asshole." Not that I hate the idea of seeing him today. "Plus, what's he supposed to do with his kids here? They'll be bored."

"That's up to him. Don't come up with reasons not to ask," Kenzie adds her two cents, and I have to begrudgingly admit she's not wrong.

"But what if I look needy?" I ask in all seriousness, and Maddox laughs at me.

"You're the least needy girl in this room, evil twin."

Two pillows fly at his head from opposite sides of the room as Brynn and Kenzie both yell at him. Cross did invite me to his house. I guess it would be nice if I gave up a little of my control and at least extended an invitation, right? I mean, it's not like he's going to really come with both kids.

I ignore the looks the three of them throw at me when I get up and walk into the kitchen to FaceTime Cross. The

THE WILDCAT

screen lights up, and he answers right away, his dark eyes shining. "Hey, Cinderella."

"Hey, big man. Your house sounds quiet." Brynn yells at Maddox in the other room, and I stifle a laugh.

"Yours doesn't." Cross's crooked smile does wicked things to me.

"Yeah well, we like to watch the Kings games together when the team is away. I thought maybe you'd like to come over and watch with us. You could bring the kids. But I totally understand if you don't want to. I mean..."

"You inviting me over to your house, Everly?" His tone is teasingly low and sexy.

"We're loud and obnoxious. And if you bring the kids, I can't promise they won't hear cursing." Geez, I'm really selling the hell out of this.

"You sure you want my kids too?" Oh, this man. He's put himself out there for me, and he's not sure if I want him to bring his kids. I'm an asshole.

"Yeah, Wilder. Bring the kids. I can ask Lindy to bring stuff for Jax, if it makes it easier." I'm already wondering how fast Target could deliver a few things. "Does Kerrigan like pizza? Bellamy and Ares are welcome to come too. We're super low-key for home games. It starts in a half an hour."

"We'll be there. Do you need me to pick anything up?"

"Nope. See you soon, Cross." I end the call and drop my head back against the cabinet. "Brynn, we're going to need to order more food."

Our doorman buzzes Cross up just before kickoff, and I've got to say, I'm pretty proud of myself. In the time it took Cross to get here, Maddox had West End deliver more food. Also Lindy and Easton have come upstairs with Griffin, and they brought a pack-n-play and a little exerciser thing that's still way too big for Griffin but Easton said might work for Jax. And Leo called to say he was coming over too, so I told him to stop and grab more beer. I also told him if he brings Hendrix to not let him fangirl over Cross. Not sure if it will work or not, but it's worth a shot.

If Cross thought his house was a shit show, he ain't seen nothing yet.

I open the door and smile when I see him. Cross is carrying Jax in one arm and holding Kerrigan's hand with the other. He leans down and kisses my cheek as soon as he sees me. "You ready for this?"

The words are quiet. Just for me. And I'm not sure why, but I love that he asked.

"I am, but you may not be." I step aside, and Kerrigan clings to Cross. "Hi, sweet girl." I squat down to her level and lower my voice. "There's lots of people here, but you know what?"

She shakes her head.

"They're all my friends. And two of my brothers are here. Do you want to meet them?"

She looks to her father, like I'm learning Kerrigan always does first, and waits for his nod, before she takes my hand. I decide to take a chance and scoop her up so she's sitting on my hip, and then this little girl steals my heart. She wraps her arms around my neck and starts playing with my hair. Yup. I'm a goner.

We walk into the loud family room at the very end of the national anthem, and you can suddenly hear a pin drop because every single person in the room stops talking and stares. *Way to make it weird, guys.* "Guys, I'd like you to meet my new friends. This is Kerrigan and Jax. And that's Ares and Cross."

One beat passes, then another before Kerrigan hides her face in my hair.

"Don't worry, sweets. I've got you," I tell her as I watch my shithead brothers make a beeline for Cross and Ares.

Why are boys so stupid?

I move over to the girls and introduce Kerrigan to baby Griffin, who's much more her speed, and watch Cross over her head as he stares at me. It's getting harder to remember why I'm not supposed to fall for this man.

Cross

"I'm surprised to see you here, man," Everly's brother Leo tells me as he hands me a beer.

What the fuck am I supposed to say to that?

"I just mean, evil twin doesn't usually bring guys around the family."

Yeah . . . and now I'm glad I'm holding Jax. It would really suck if I hit Everly's brother.

"Thanks, man. Appreciate it." I move around him, and he groans.

"That's not what I meant."

Okay. I'm game. I turn around and wait.

"Evil twin is picky. She likes her friends and her family and doesn't ever bring people into her inner circle. She *never* brings guys in. That's a good thing for you. I might not have said it all flowery and shit, but it was meant as a good thing."

"You always call your sister evil?" I fucking hate it, and they all do it.

He shrugs. "It's her nickname." The front door closes, and Leo looks around me. "Good twin just got home."

"Yeah. Those nicknames suck." I walk away and see Kerrigan's confused little eyes bouncing like a pinball between Everly and her sister.

"Cross," Everly calls to me, and I move as if being pulled by an invisible string. "Cross Wilder, I'd like to introduce you to my other half, my sister, Grace."

"It's so nice to meet you, Cross," Grace offers and then reaches out. "Could I hold the baby?"

"Sure. But fair warning. He's cranky," I tell her as Ares moves in next to us.

"Dude. There's two of them." He doesn't even bother to whisper, and Everly and Grace both glare.

"You're an asshole," I mutter, but Ares keeps going.

"Did you guys ever, ya know . . . switch places?"

At least that's all he asks, because I thought he was going somewhere else with that question. "Why did I bring you?"

"We did it a few times growing up. No one could ever tell us apart." Everly smiles like she's remembering a funny story she can't share in front of little ears.

"You guys used to try that shit every summer," the bartender grunts.

"And you'd fall for it every time," Grace laughs.

The bartender, whose name I know but I'd rather ignore, crosses his arms over his chest. "You're identical twins. Of course we'd fall for it. It was impossible to tell you apart."

Dumbass. I run my thumb over Everly's cheek. It's been minutes, and I can already tell them apart. "You have a freckle on your cheek." I look over again at Grace. "Yours is on your right cheek. Grace's is on her left."

Ares laughs, and bartender boy stares like he's never noticed before. Maybe he really doesn't have a thing for my girl.

Maybe I'll start using his name.

"They used to wear more makeup," he grunts.

Grace runs her hand over Jax's back as he snuggles in against her chest, then she cups Maddox's cheek with the same hand. "We've never worn that much makeup, Madman, but nice try." She turns to me and flashes a smile so similar to her sister's, it's almost eerie. "I knew you were one of the good ones."

Grace hands Jax off to Everly, who's never held my son before. "I'm going to go shower and change. Practice was awful today, and my whole body hurts."

"You need any help in the shower?" Ares asks Grace, and she's polite enough to just laugh, not tell my idiot brother off.

Everly, on the other hand, looks like she's contemplating his death.

"You want to die, God of War?" Yup—contemplating his death. I was right.

He puts his hands up in front of himself, and I think I hear Maddox growl. Then the strangest thing happens. As if in slo-mo, Kerrigan moves in front of Maddox and grabs his hand.

My daughter, who doesn't talk to strangers.

"It's okay. Daddy says Uncle Ares gets hit in the head too many times, and ice is hard. We have to be nice to him."

The dude looks like he's about to choke on his laughter, but he mans up and doesn't laugh at my kid, who's clearly very serious right now. Instead, he lays his arm across the back of the couch, where he and Kerrigan are both sitting, and watches as she scooches closer to him. "Your uncle is lucky to have you watching his back."

She nods silently and settles in next to him, like some kind of alternate reality where she likes strangers. I stand there, stuck in place for a few beats before turning to my brother. "Do you ever think before you speak?"

Ares looks less than impressed. "What the fuck, dude? Too many hits to the head?"

"Be grateful that's all I told her."

He walks away, sulking.

Everly laughs as she steps into me, her beautiful body swaying to a silent beat to soothe my son. "I swear, I didn't know everyone was going to be here today when I invited you. I hope this is okay."

I wrap my arms around her waist, dragging her even closer, and press my lips against her forehead. "It's all good, baby."

She sighs a happy sigh, and her shoulders loosen like she needed the contact as much as I did.

Jax takes that as a sign and yanks a fistful of her hair, unintentionally forcing us to look over at Maddox, who's laughing at my daughter's obsession with something on TV.

"I swear to God, Kerrigan is usually shy. The fact that she talked to you the other night at the house was a miracle. This . . . this is just weird."

Everly hums against Jax's hand. "Madman always has a way with the ladies."

"You know I really wanted to hate him," I tell her, enjoying the happy look on her face.

"I told you." She kisses Jax's hand again. "He's like a brother."

"I'm way more sane than your brothers, evil twin," Maddox calls back, clearly having heard every word we said.

"Yeah . . . I had a talk with your brother." I stand back, watching Everly charm Jaxon. He's half in love already, and I'm tempted to say, *yeah, kid, same*. "Leo mentioned you don't bring people around your family."

"I don't," she tells me before lifting up on her toes until her lips skim my ear, ignoring the fact we're in a room full of people. "I told you I wanted to try, Cross. And I meant it. This is me trying. I've got no clue what I'm doing, and you scare me to death. But I'm still trying. Just try to remember that when I mess it all up, okay?"

She tries to take a step back, but I tighten my hold and tug her closer. "Your time, Cinderella."

I press my lips against hers until Jax shoves his fat fingers into my eye, prying us apart.

"Guess the little man doesn't like to share." Her sweet voice wraps around me like a fucking blanket. Comforting and reassuring. Hearing her coo at my kids. The way she seems to have taken to both of them and the way they've taken to her. I didn't know how I'd feel about any of this because I never imagined being a single father until I was one. And even then, dating wasn't my priority. Probably would have stayed that way if I hadn't met her.

"Neither does his dad."

"Get a room," Hendrix yells, and the room erupts around us.

These fuckers are crazy.

"You remember that story about those kids following the pervy piper out of Australia?" Ares asks later that night, while I stand back in the living room, watching both my kids sleep on Everly.

"You make it really hard sometimes, brother. You know that, right?"

"What the hell?" And the scary thing is he's serious.

"It was the pied piper, and he led the snakes out of Ireland." I look around at what's left of the party. My girl may have sworn up and down this was just a regular game, but she had over ten people here and enough food to feed twenty. That's a party.

"Whatever. I always thought he put the kids in a trance. I was gonna say that's kind of what your girl has done. I've never seen Kerrigan so taken with anyone before. And no offense to Everly, but she's got boobs, and Jax is a boob man. The minute his head hit those, he was a happy baby. So she's got a fan for life in him." Ares smacks my back. "Anyway, I'm getting out of here. I'll see you at home."

"We've got our first preseason game this week, man. Don't do anything stupid." If Kingston needs me to step up, a great place to start will have to be with my own brother. "Coach will kick all our asses if you guys get caught fucking up again."

"I wasn't doing anything stupid last time. I was just along for the ride," he argues. "And I won't do anything tonight either. Just stopping by Boone's before I head home."

"Are you okay to drive?" Everly asks him as she joins us, having left the kids with Grace on the couch.

"I only had two beers, blondie. I'm fine. Thanks for having me tonight." He wraps an arm around her for a quick hug, then leaves.

Guess he's not always an ass.

I tuck her hair behind both ears and drop a kiss on her forehead. "Did you have a good time?"

I can feel her smile before I see it. "Shouldn't I be asking you that?"

"You're happy, and my kids are happy. It's a good day."

Her lips brush my chin. "One of these days, it's going to be a good night too, Cross."

"Yeah, baby." I catch her lips with mine. "One of these nights."

EVERLY

I lay my head down against my knees, grab my feet, and flex my toes, enjoying the warm stretch of my muscles after our last three-hour dance practice before this weekend's game. Our next game is *Monday Night Football* against the team we lost the championship to last year. So the networks are making a huge deal out of it. That always puts Miss Cassabian into a tizzy. She's been Kings cheerleading for twenty years, and she definitely missed her calling. She would have made a hell of a drill sergeant in another life.

She stands next to me, waiting as everyone else files out. "Plan on going home tonight, Miss Sinclair?"

My guilty conscious eats at me, but I pull myself up and slide my Uggs on. "Sorry, Miss Cassabian. My quad was bothering me a little, so I wanted to make sure I really stretched it out." I grab my dance bag from the floor and throw my hoodie over my tank. "See you Monday."

"Are you going to see that hockey beau of yours?" She follows behind me, shutting off the lights and locking the door.

"Miss C, you pay too much attention to the Kroydon

Kronicles. I don't have a new beau. And if I did, he'd be playing in a preseason game right now anyway." A game he may have invited me to. Not that I feel guilty for skipping it. I mean, I can't skip cheer practice for it. We're only allowed to miss so many practices without being benched for a game. But I haven't missed a single one this season. I probably could have asked to come late to this practice if I really wanted to.

"If you say so, dear. But I'd check your phone. The game's over. The team lost," she adds as I get into my car and do exactly what she said. I pull my phone out and google the Revolution. Cross scored once. Jace Kingston scored once. But Easton let in three goals. So they lost by one. Damn. Wouldn't want to be Lindy when Easton gets home tonight.

Wouldn't want to be Bellamy either. Cross and Ares are probably both miserable, if they're anything like my family. Dad was never great at shaking off the losses. He wouldn't take it out on us or anything at all like that. But he'd definitely take them out on himself. Mom was so happy when he retired last year.

Without overthinking it too much, I turn toward my parent's house instead of our condo. Not long afterward, I pull into their driveway. Making sure to knock loudly before just letting myself in—because there's an old family story about Grandpa and Grandma getting caught naked in their kitchen. And nobody needs their own repeat of that.

I knock once more, just to be sure, then I let myself in. "Mom..." I call out.

"In the kitchen," she answers, and Dad pops his head out of his office.

"Hey, Evie. I didn't know you were stopping by tonight."

"Hi, Daddy. I needed to talk to Mom about something." I stop by his door and kiss his cheek before making my way back to their kitchen. "Hey, Mom. Hey, Aunt Nat."

"Hey, kid," Aunt Nattie pats the seat next to her, then squeezes me when I sit down.

Mom takes another mug from the shelf and adds a tea bag to it before pouring hot water from the kettle and sitting it in front of me. "I was just making us a cup of tea. Do you want one?"

"It's not decaf, right?"

"Daughter dearest, do you know me at all? The only bad part about being pregnant with all of you was giving up caffeine. And it was the only time in my life I'm ever going to do that. Now sit and tell me why you're here."

"Do I need to have a reason?" I add a few scoops of sugar and sip my tea.

Aunt Nattie laughs. "Yes. You forget we were your age once."

Mom smiles. "Well, you're drinking caffeine, so at least I know you're not pregnant."

"Mother," I gasp. "Really?"

Nattie and she snicker behind their cups.

"Fine, I'd have to be having sex to be pregnant, and that's not happening. So no, it's safe to say I'm not pregnant." I decide to add another spoonful of sugar, then look around her counter. "Do you have any sweets?"

"Seriously . . . do you know your mother at all?" Nattie feigns shock.

Mom pulls a carton of mint chocolate chip out of the freezer, then grabs three spoons.

"Ice cream and hot tea?" I ask as she hands out the spoons, and we tap them together like we've always done before digging in. "Why not?"

After a mouthful of minty chip goodness, I look across the counter at the way they're both patiently waiting for me to spill my guts. "What are you two up to?"

"I was plotting my next book and wanted your mom's

advice. Your turn. What's his name? What did he do? And can I use it in my next book?"

"Why does it have to be a guy?" I protest pitifully.

"You're in my kitchen, eating ice cream from a carton on a Saturday night instead of out with the girls," Mom says, and Aunt Nattie nods in agreement.

"Fine. It's Cross," I tell the two of them and shove another spoonful in my mouth.

"Ohh . . . the hockey player?" Nattie turns her head to Mom. "The single dad?"

"Yeah, that's him," Mom agrees, and I smack the counter.

"What the heck, Mom? You told the whole family?"

"No," she protests, but I can tell from the guilty look on her face she totally did. "Okay, fine. I may have mentioned it to Nat, and Amelia and Carys already knew."

Nattie raises her spoon. "I told Sabrina and Catherine."

"Grandma knows?" I gasp. "That is the definition of the entire family, Mom."

"In my defense, your brother came over with his dirty laundry and mentioned that Cross and his kids were at your condo for the Kings game last week, and I got excited."

"And drunk," Nattie adds. "That was the night last week with those margaritas during book club."

Oh great. Book club is basically when my mom and all my aunts get together to act like they're talking about books, but really they're talking about sex and testing out whatever new cocktail recipe one of them saw on Instagram that week.

And they were talking about me.

"It was," Mom agrees, and I drop my arms on the counter and lay my forehead down on them.

"Do you think maybe we could focus here?" I mumble from behind my arms. "You two haven't been sneaking the tequila into your tea, have you?"

"No, dear. Whiskey goes in tea."

THE WILDCAT

My mother, ladies and gentlemen.

She wasn't always this crazy. It's probably partially my fault. Maybe one-fifth my fault, if we split her craziness between the kids.

I lift my eyes without moving my head from my arms and look at these women. My mom and my aunt. Two women who married professional athletes. Quarterbacks at the top of their games. And both have disgustingly happy marriages. At least, based on how many kids they each have and how many times they've gotten caught doing naughty things with their husbands on family vacations. Still not as bad as Grandpa and Grandma though.

My eyes may never recover, and I've never even seen it.

"I really like this guy. He listens to what I say. Really hears it and doesn't just act like he's paying attention while he looks at my boobs. He's a gentleman. And his kids. He's so good with his kids. And he stops by the shop with coffee, just to see me for a few minutes after practice. It's just a few minutes, but I look forward to it each day. And he doesn't push. Not at all. Like he's just so sure it's going to happen when it's supposed to happen that he's not worried about it. Why can't I be like that?" I ask, frustrated beyond belief. "I'm falling hard, and I'm petrified."

I finally admit it and stab the ice cream, waiting for one of them to give me some pearls of wisdom. But they don't say anything. Nothing. Not a single word. They both just stare. "Well? Aren't you going to tell me I'm being stupid?"

"Do *you* think you're being stupid?" Nattie asks. "I don't think you do. I think you're nervous, and that makes sense—because this is a different type of relationship for you."

"What scares you, Everly?" Mom asks, and I try to figure out how to verbalize the answer.

"I've dated athletes before—"

"Stop," Nattie cuts me off. "Just because two people are

athletes doesn't mean they have a single thing in common, other than being an athlete. Don't lump this man in with an ex who was an athlete just because they both play a sport."

"Honey." Mom drops her spoon in the sink and moves around the counter to sit next to me. "What your aunt is trying to say is what you're doing isn't fair. Yes, some athletes are jerks and terrible boyfriends. They're probably awful husbands and lousy men in general. But for every bad one, there's a good one like your father and your uncles. Those men treat us with so much respect, honey. We're their equals, their partners. Your father has put me before everything in this world for twenty-four years. I've never doubted him, and I've never regretted my decision to let myself love him."

Aunt Nattie points her spoon at me. "A good man is a good man, Evie. It doesn't matter what their career choice is. But I want you to keep this in mind. An athlete's job demands different things than a teacher or a lawyer's job does. The hours are different. The travel can be awful. The press is intrusive. And the fans think they own them. There are plenty of reasons to be hesitant to get into a relationship with an athlete." Nat reaches across the counter and grabs my hand. "But you were born into a football dynasty. You know those pitfalls. And I'd bet they don't have anything to do with your fear."

"They don't," I grumble, already knowing they're right.

My head knows it. My heart still needs to work through it.

"And if he hurts you, Uncle Sam could make him disappear," Nattie adds, and Mom laughs.

"Forget Sam. Amelia's who he should be scared of."

They're both wrong.

It's me.

I'm who Cross should be scared of.

I think I'm the one who could hurt him most if I can't get past this.

"Sweetheart, relationships are scary. But you're my fearless girl. Scary hasn't ever stopped you before. Are you going to let it now?"

Some days, I wish I could be the good twin.

Fearlessness is overrated.

CROSS

Are you going to come to the door?

CINDERELLA

What are you talking about?

CROSS

You've been parked in front of my house for thirty minutes. Either you've got something on your mind or you're casing the joint. And since your condo might be worth two of my houses, I'm thinking it's the first thing.

CINDERELLA

Technically, Lindy owns the condo. So maybe I am casing the joint. My ass would look great in one of those cat burglar suits.

CROSS

It would look better up in the air, bright red, and covered with my handprints. But that would require you coming inside.

CINDERELLA

Is that a promise?

> **CROSS**
> Thirty minutes, Cinderella. Come inside. Tell me what's on your mind. Then we'll see about the rest.

> **CINDERELLA**
> It's raining.

> **CROSS**
> Seems to be a theme for us.

> **CINDERELLA**
> Your driveway is a mile long.

> **CROSS**
> It's a quarter of a mile.
> You want an umbrella?

This is ridiculous. I pull the hood of my sweatshirt over my head and make a run for Cross's door, not slowing down until I'm under the roof of the wraparound porch, soaked and dripping wet, when Cross steps outside. He's still dressed from his game, and he looks good. So damn good. Expensive black slacks and a crisp white dress shirt highlight every sexy feature, but it's the worn baseball hat, unbuttoned collar, and rolled up sleeves, showcasing the mother of all arm porn that remind me this is my Cross. Even cleaned up, this man wants to be comfortable. He's even wearing a chunky leather watch, completely clueless about what the whole damn package that is Cross Wilder does to mere mortals like me.

"What's going on, Everly?"

"Have you ever done something you were positive was going to get you hurt?" I ask as my chest heaves, wild with adrenaline.

"You tell me. Are you about to tell me you can't do this?"

he asks, and I know that's because I'm all over the damn place. I could give a saint whiplash.

He doesn't deserve that.

I shake my head.

"Thank fuck." He crosses the porch in two strides and grabs the back of my head. "I need you to tell me you want this, baby." Cross's eyes are fixed on mine. His dark pupils, blown wide with want, send a sharp, sweet bolt of heartache through me.

We might destroy each other, but I'm not going down without a fight.

I fist the front of his shirt and lift my chin. "I want this, and I need you."

The words have barely left my lips when his strong arms wrap around me. Cross's calloused hands slide under my old worn Kings hoodie and scorch my heated skin before he lifts me from my feet and wraps my legs around his waist.

"I need you so fucking much, Everly. You're mine, baby. Mine to take care of. To protect. And I'll tell you as many times as you need to hear it."

His words are a balm to all the tattered edges of my cracked and tortured soul. The one that shattered so completely, I wasn't sure I'd ever be willing to take this step. They soothe the fear that won't stop but seems to always quiet in his presence.

Cross walks us around the side of the house until we're hidden on the back of the wraparound porch and sits us down on a chaise lounge big enough for three people.

I tug off his cap and run my fingers through his dark hair. "Didn't want to go inside?"

"I like the rain" is all he says before he pulls my face down to his and takes my mouth in a kiss I feel everywhere. "Kids are asleep. Ares is out, and Bellamy's crashing at Caitlin's. We've got the house to ourselves."

The rain beats down on the roof above us and plays the prettiest tune as it hits the lake in the distance. The bright moon illuminates Cross just enough for me to see his onyx eyes scan every inch of my face. "You want to tell me why you sat in front of my house for thirty minutes?"

"There are other things I'd rather be doing." I press my lips to the corner of his mouth and revel in the touch of his hands on my bare skin under my hoodie. His hands make slow passes up and down my rib cage. He never goes further than the band of my dance shorts or the bottom of my sports bra. Each tortuous stroke making it harder to think.

"Everly . . ."

"I don't trust easily, Cross. I've been hurt. And before you ask, no, I don't want to talk about it now. But you . . . It's like my heart knows I can trust you. And if it makes any sense at all, my brain knows it too. But man, the fear is still there. The fear is louder than everything else."

"Baby, you've got nothing to fear. Not from me. Never from me. I'm not that guy."

His hand moves up the tiniest bit farther on its next pass up my ribs, and I shiver under his touch. "I don't like to be vulnerable, and you make me feel that way. I'm not sure I'd ever be able to put the pieces back together after you."

"Then it's a good thing I'm never letting you go." His tongue slides along my lips, and I moan as he pushes it inside my mouth. "Mine, Everly."

Thunder crashes in the distance, followed by a bright bolt of lightning as the rain picks up around us, cocooning us in our own small piece of the world. I arch into his touch, and Cross finally slides his hand under my bra. His rough hand cups my breast, and those deliciously calloused fingers pinch my nipple, leaving me aching. Needing more.

"Cross . . ." I beg as I slide my legs to straddle either side of his lap, desperate to feel him.

I wrap my hands around his head, my fingers tugging on his hair, as our tongues tangle, fighting for control.

Finally . . . *finally*, he pulls back and rips my hoodie up over my head.

My hair falls down in waves, and Cross sucks in a sharp breath. "I fucking love your hair, Cinderella."

I laugh at the ridiculous use of that nickname and play with the top button of his shirt until I pop each one open and press my palms flat against his chest. "I've dreamed of you naked since July, Cross. You've got on way too many clothes."

Cross's silent laughter makes me smile. "At least I'm dressed. What the hell are you wearing?"

"Dance shorts and a sports bra. It's what I practice in."

"Fuck, baby. My boxers cover more than those." His hands run up my thighs as he bites down on my bottom lip and tugs. "Do you have on panties under them?" One hand slides from my hip into my booty shorts and under my thong. I'm about to say I guess he got his answer when his fingers drag through my drenched sex. The palm of his hand presses against my clit, sending me spiraling through the storm.

"Fucking drenched." His eyes find mine and hold them as he teases my entrance. "Is this pussy needy for me?" he growls.

"I've pictured you every time I fucked myself for months, Cross." I drag my lips over the scruff of his jaw until they skim his ear. "You already own this pussy."

Cross throws his head back against the chair and moans as he pushes one blunt finger inside me. Then another. "Fuck, Everly . . ."

His rough thumb rubs circles around my clit, teasing me as I drag my tongue down the column of his neck and bite down on his shoulder. So fucking close to flying.

Cool chills coat my skin as Cross's fingers curve to hit a

spot deep inside while he presses down on my clit. My universe shrinks to just the two of us locked in this moment.

My core tightens, and my body lights up.

Cross licks into my mouth. "You gonna be a good girl and come for me, Everly?"

I nod my head and get lost in the crackling heat dancing in his dark eyes.

"You gotta be quiet, baby. Can you be quiet?"

A whimper slips past my lips, and Cross crushes his mouth to mine, swallowing my moan. The possessiveness of his kiss and the way he knows just how to touch me send me catapulting over the edge.

He pulls his fingers out, and I whimper again at the sudden loss, still utterly blissed-out. He traces my lips with his fingers, and I suck them into my mouth, my tongue swirling around his fingers before he kisses me. "Such a good fucking girl."

Cross pulls away and leans back in the chair, then grips my hips with a wicked grin and slides me over his face.

"Cross..."

"Shh... just a taste." He pulls my shorts and thong down, and I wiggle out of them carefully. I immediately moan at the exquisite pleasure of Cross Wilder's mouth on me.

"Such a pretty pussy, Everly."

Holy shit. I didn't think I could get hotter.

I rip my bra off and toss it to the floor, then grip the back of the chair and try to catch my breath.

Fuck it. I don't need to breathe.

Cross drags his flattened tongue through my pussy like I'm his favorite fucking dessert. Then... Oh God... his stubble... his tongue. His fucking fingers.

He growls against my sex, sending vibrations through my core, and I think I might come again.

I throw my head back, trying desperately to stay quiet.

To stay locked in our own private world where nothing else can touch us.

I should be horrified at how wet I am, but when his lips wrap around my clit and he slides two fingers into my pussy and . . . holy shit . . . another in my ass, I lose the ability to think, or care, or breathe.

Breathing is overrated.

My entire body becomes one giant electric pulse, stronger than any lightning strike.

"Give me one more, Everly."

Darkness clouds my vision. And when I think I can't take it anymore . . . when I might die from lack of oxygen, his teeth finally scrape over my throbbing clit, and I detonate.

Breathless.

Soundless.

Completely lost and suddenly strangely found as I stare into his eyes, with a new need.

CROSS

Everly drops her forehead to mine and closes her eyes. "You make me feel everything, Cross. Things I don't want to feel."

When she looks up, my gorgeous girl takes my breath away. Her golden-blonde hair spills around us, blocking out the stormy skies above us. It's just her and me and the rain. I pull the baby monitor out of my pocket and drop it to the floor, then kiss her. Because I can't not kiss her. "So fucking pretty, baby. So pretty and so mine."

"I *am* yours, Cross." Her smile is small and beautiful before she carefully moves off my lap and kneels between my legs. Those aquamarine eyes I dream about look up at me through impossibly long, dark lashes. Her sun-kissed skin shimmers in the moonlight. She's fucking perfection. "Now I need to make *you* mine."

Fuck . . .

"You're fucking right, I'm yours. And I don't share, Everly. Not with anyone. Not even a past that haunts you. You're gonna let me in one day, so I can destroy those demons for you."

She beams back at me, like I just gave her the world, and I make a silent vow to destroy whoever hurt her.

Everly's eyes stay locked on mine while she unbuckles my belt and works my pants and boxers down.

My cock springs free, and my girl licks her lips and wraps her fist around me.

My muscles coil tight, and I gather her soft hair in my hands, needing to see her.

Her ocean-colored eyes are glazed and hungry.

So fucking needy.

"Put me in your mouth, baby," I growl, and her smile grows.

"Patience, Cross. It's my turn." She drags her tongue from the base of my cock all the way up to the swollen head. She licks the pearl of precum with a flick, then wraps her pouty pink lips around me, and *fuck* . . . I could die happy like this.

My blood thickens, and my spine pulls tight at the first fucking feel of her warm, wet mouth. I cup her face in my hand and run my thumb along her jaw. "I can be patient," I remind her.

Her lashes flutter, and her lips part on a sexy fucking sigh as she swallows me down the back of her throat.

Fuuuuccckkk . . .

Patience I can do. But with her mouth on me, restraint is way fucking harder.

Everly's head bobs, and her eyes water as she works her way up and down my cock, humming around me. The vibrations drive me crazy. Her tongue. Her mouth. Her eyes locked on mine. Everything about her drives me fucking crazy. And I'm here for all of it.

But this isn't how I'm gonna come. Not tonight. I need inside my girl.

I pull her hair and tug her to my lap. "The first time I have you, I'm coming inside your pussy, baby. Not in your mouth."

"You've already had me, Cross," she pouts, but she still wraps her arms and legs around me so my cock is nestled against her sex. And fuck me, even that feels like heaven.

"I had your body before. Now I want the rest of you. But I've got to go grab a condom first. I didn't exactly think to put one in my pocket when I thought you were sitting in front of my house ready to end things." I lift her so I can get up, but she pushes me back down.

"Cross . . ." she whispers, dragging her fingers down my face. "I'm on the shot. I'm clean, and we're safe. I just want to feel you. Nothing between us."

What she's not saying speaks louder than any words ever could.

"You sure?" I run my hand up her ribs and wrap it around her throat, then press my thumb over her thrumming pulse. "Because once you let me inside you bare, I'm not letting you go, baby."

"Don't let go, Cross. Even when I run. Don't let go."

Everly reaches between us and drags my cock through her soaked sex. Her smile takes my breath away as she lifts up on her knees and fists a hand around my cock, fitting me against her hot, wet cunt as she slowly lowers herself over me.

She inches down slowly, her whimpers filling the air as she stretches to take me in.

So fucking tight.

So fucking mine.

This girl . . . I don't know what fucking spell she's woven, but I'm never letting go.

Wide eyes hold mine as I wrap my arm around her, my fingers biting into the soft skin of her round ass. "You look so pretty, baby. Taking my cock like such a good girl."

She breathes out and drags her nails up my back, scoring my skin. Her earlier orgasm still dripping between us as her gorgeous eyes flutter closed, and she finally starts to move.

"Eyes on me, Everly."

Her eyes fly to mine as she wraps her arms around my shoulders and clings to me, picking up her speed and taking me deeper until she's shaking and panting and chanting my name.

That's when the final fraying thread of control I'm desperately clinging to snaps, and there's nothing holding me back.

Slamming my lips over hers, I swallow her moans as I fuck into her, over and over.

Hitting that rough, sweet, hidden spot inside if her. Building us up higher and higher until there's nowhere left to go. No space between us. Just the two of us.

Nothing has ever felt so fucking good in my life.

"Oh, God. Cross . . ." Everly throws her head back, her long hair kissing the tops of my thighs, as she arches her back and claws at my shoulders. Her flawless fucking tits and pretty pink nipples are peaked and perfect and begging to be sucked. She moans as I wrap my mouth around one and slam her body back down over mine. Going so deep, I see fucking stars.

My muscles tighten with every sharp snap of my hips, every drip of her earlier orgasm sliding over my cock. Every sexy moan that falls from her lips.

I want to keep her.

To claim her.

To make sure she feels me between her legs for fucking days.

All fucking mine.

White-hot blistering heat pools at the base of my spine as a fiery, all-consuming need threatens to burn the world down around us, and we fuck our way into oblivion.

We lie limp in a tangle of limbs and legs long after we come down from our high. Everly's head rests on my chest while I play with her hair. The cool, damp air dances over our hot bodies. Neither of us talking. No words are needed until goosebumps pebble her skin. "You're getting cold, Cinderella. I think we better take this inside."

She lifts her head up and rests her chin on my chest, a mischievous look on her face. "I don't think I'll ever look at rain the same way."

I drag a hand down the bumps of her spine and gently smack her perfect fucking ass. "I've always loved the rain. The way it washes everything away. I love the way it smells. The way it feels. Growing up, I loved that it would turn to ice. Ice we could skate on at the lake in the center of town. But I gotta tell you, I've never loved it more than tonight."

The baby monitor crackles, picking up Jax's pained whimper.

"Shit. I gotta check on him. His molars are coming in, and he's running a low-grade fever." I press my lips to her forehead and grab my boxers from the floor. "You gonna be here when I get back?"

She nods but doesn't give me any words. Lost in her head again.

I feel her eyes on me as I walk inside and wonder if she's going to bolt.

She asked me not to let go even when she runs.

I guess she hasn't realized I'm not going anywhere.

Unless it's to chase her.

Everly

Don't leave.

Damn. Those words play over in my mind and make me feel awful. He thinks I'd run, even after tonight. I can't even be mad because my head is telling me to run as far and as fast as I can.

Because after that...

Being that honest.

Making myself that vulnerable.

I'm not sure where that leaves me. Leaves us. *Shit.* He's right. I was thinking about ending things earlier. Self-preservation is a bitch. And she's telling me I won't survive Cross Wilder.

The monitor crackles again, and I hear Cross's voice as he attempts to soothe Jax.

"Hey, buddy. Come here," he coos in his calming voice. "Not feeling so good, huh?"

Jax's cries pick up, and Cross sighs. "All right, all right. Let's get you changed, then we'll go find a bottle, okay? Maybe if we're lucky, Cinderella will still be here when we get back downstairs."

I grab his shirt off the ground and throw it on, then pick up the rest of our mess and head inside to look for something to drink... Something warm.

The kettle's whistling and I'm eating a cookie I found in the cabinet by the time Cross walks into the kitchen with Jax in his arms. Yup. I've got a daddy kink. It's official. Because my man—bare-chested with his baby in light-blue footie pajamas and curled up on Cross's big, broad, bare chest—is fucking stunning. Holy hot daddy.

I want that.

"Found the cookies?" he teases, and I nod. "Guess that chocolate cake cleanse ended?"

"I decided life's too short to not enjoy cake . . . and cookies. All things sweet, really. I was eating ice cream out of a carton with my mom and aunt earlier. Thank goodness for good genes, or I'd be the size of a house."

Cross eyes his shirt hanging off me. It's so big. A cocky grin slides across his face before he brushes his lips over mine. "You look good in my clothes, Cinderella."

"Mm-hmm . . ." I hum because words are hard when your ovaries are inexplicably exploding. And your heart . . . well, that's doing other things.

"Can you hold him for me while I make a bottle?"

He doesn't wait for an answer before handing me Jax, who immediately tangles my hair around his chubby little fist and lays his head on my chest.

I walk the two of us into the other room, while Cross makes Jax's bottle in the kitchen. The storm has picked up, and I stop in front of a wall of floor-to-ceiling windows to watch the lightning over the lake.

"Oh, buddy . . ." I rub a hand soothingly over his back as his heavy breathing slows. "Giving my heart to your daddy scares me. But you . . . You just took it without my permission."

My little white swan pops her head up. *You know . . .* she starts, and my black swan flicks her right off my shoulder. *Don't go there, little miss perfect.*

Tired of the voices in my head, I think I close them both off for the last time and hum and old song my mom used to have us warm up to as I sway gently, hopefully calming my poor little buddy.

Cross's heavy footsteps catch my attention before I feel him move in behind me.

"You know, you look really good holding my son, Everly. Not many things scare me. I'm just not that guy. But the idea of letting you in their lives and then them possibly losing you too . . ." He stares at me for a long minute. And I feel like I'm holding my breath, waiting for his next words. "That's fucking terrifying."

I sit down on the couch, and Cross hands me Jax's bottle, then walks out of the room.

I remember when my youngest cousins were born. Grace and I had our very own doll babies. We were old enough to enjoy them but not to appreciate how holding a baby makes you feel. Jax's dark eyes, every bit the same as his father's, focus on me as he takes his first few pulls of the bottle before they grow heavy and soon close.

"I've got three back-to-back away games this week, then one home and another away game next week before the season really kicks in." Cross comes back in with two cups of tea and holds one out for me.

"Would you mind just putting it down. I don't want to move and wake him."

He laughs a short, quiet sound. "Amateur."

"Yeah well, I haven't had seven months of practice. Dating a daddy wasn't in my plans. Dating an athlete wasn't in my plans either. I don't date, Cross. I don't do this."

"Sorry," he says softly, and I feel like a shit.

"I know. I didn't mean it like that. It's just . . . I'm not sure how I feel about going to your games." I'm also not sure I'm ready to talk about this yet, but I don't add that.

His brow shoots up. "You never went to a hockey game with Madeline Kingston?"

"I haven't gone to a boyfriend's game in a long time," I answer softly.

Cross sits next to me and wraps an arm around my shoulders. "Boyfriend, huh?"

"Really? That's what you got out of that?" I catch the edge of my lip between my teeth and look away. "What exactly am I supposed to call you after all that outside and now . . . ?" I look down at Jax, who has milk dripping out of the corner of his mouth. "And now, all this in here? Pretty sure we're past just friends with benefits, Wilder."

Cross tangles his hand in my hair and massages my scalp.

And it feels divine.

"We were never just friends, Everly."

It's my turn to look skeptical.

"I knew there was something special about you the night we met. I spent years with Helene." When I make a face, he adds, "Their mom."

"Oh."

"Hear me out, baby. I spent years with her and never felt for her what I felt for you the first night we met. What does that tell you? Because it sure as shit tells me you matter. And we were never just friends. I'm trying to give you the space you need. The time. The control. I might be arrogant, but I'm not stupid. And I know you're a flight risk. I also know you're hung up on my career, even if I don't have a fucking clue why."

His strong hand continues its delicious massage at the base of my skull, and I want so badly to ignore what he's saying and just focus on the way his hand feels on my body. But Cross deserves more than that. He deserves a woman who's going to wear his jersey and scream his name every time he sets a skate on the ice.

"I wasn't trying to guilt you in to coming to one of my games. I was trying to include you in my life because it's about to get crazy complicated. You're used to football season. They have one game a week. I can play four, sometimes five games a week. Half of them are away. And I want to know you're going to be here when I get home. I don't give a shit if you ever come to a game. You and me . . . we're not for show. I don't care if the world knows your mine. So long as *you* do."

I rest my head on his shoulder and close my eyes.

"Have I told you I love your arrogance?"

He presses his lips to my head, and a warmth washes over me.

This man . . .

The Philly Press

KROYDON KRONICLES

THE BOMBSHELL & THE BROODY BEAST

A little birdie told me Everly Sinclair was spotted sneaking out of a certain broody hockey player's house, like a thief in the night, a few days ago. Unfortunately for all of us, this reporter hasn't been able to get a picture of Kroydon Hills newest royal couple. Trust me, it's not for lack of trying. The hunt is on, beautiful people. What do we think of WildSin for their name?

#KroydonKronicles #WildSin

CROSS

"Ares, I swear to God if you make me late, I'm going to kill you," I yell up the stairs to my brother, who asked for a ride today since his car is in the shop.

"That's not nice, Daddy," Kerrigan whispers from where she's sitting on my hip.

"I'm sorry, baby girl. But Daddy is supposed to be stepping up this season, and it's going to look bad if I'm late for the flight." I kiss her temple and hold her for as long as I can. Leaving the kids never gets easier. And a three-game stretch over the next five days is fucking miserable.

Mrs. Ashburn, the kids' nanny, puts her arms out for Kerrigan. "Come here, Miss K. We talked about this. Daddy has to go to work, but he'll call you every day. And when will he be home?"

Kerrigan wiggles, and I place her on her feet so she can run over to the calendar and point to the red circle. "Here. Daddy will be home here."

"That's right," Mrs. Ashburn tells her and takes her hand. "Now why don't you and I go check on your brother and let

Daddy go to work? The sooner he goes, the sooner he comes back."

"Love you, Daddy."

I squat down and hug her again. "Love you too, baby girl. Be good for Mrs. A and Auntie Bellamy."

I stay there, watching as they walk out of the kitchen, and my idiot brother finally walks in. "Well let's go, man. I thought you were in a rush."

Some days, I think I have three kids under my roof.

The two of us pile into my truck for the short drive to the private airport the team uses. "You want to tell me what crawled up your ass and died, brother?"

"You want to tell me when you're gonna get serious about something in your life, brother?" I answer him with a definite bite to my tone. "You know, Coach and management are watching you. They're watching all of you. And you don't seem to care. You fucks were all out again last night," I growl, pissed-off that he doesn't see he could be throwing away his career.

"What does it matter that we were out? No one got hurt. No one was out of control. No bad press. We listened," Ares snaps back, pissed. "Your name was the only one splashed across social media today, Cross. Not mine."

I grind my teeth because he's not fucking wrong.

"What's really wrong, brother?"

When I don't answer, the asshole laughs. "Don't like when the tables are turned, do ya? Come on. What's going on? And when was blondie at the house? How did I miss that?"

"Last weekend, after the game. She left before you got home," I grumble.

"So . . . what's going on with you two? Come on. Who else you gonna talk to? Bellamy? She's probably having more sex than either one of us right now."

I choke on my own spit. "What the fuck, man?"

"Come on. You don't really think little sister isn't getting her rocks off when she spends the night on campus, do you?"

A dull throb starts at the base of my skull. "Jesus Christ, there's something seriously wrong with you. You know that, right?"

"Whatever. I'm just saying, there's no way you'd be wound this fucking tight if blondie was giving it up on the regular. So talk. What the hell is going on with you two?"

My grip tightens on the wheel. "I'd drop you where you were standing if I wasn't driving right now, asshat."

"Yeah, well you're driving, and I'm not standing."

Fucker.

"I don't know . . . Everly runs hot and cold. She's got some stuff to work through, but she isn't ready to talk about it. Pretty sure she hates that I play hockey."

"She knows that's kinda who you are, right? Like, you're going to be a first ballot hall of famer when you retire, and you're only thirty. You've got a shit-ton more time left to play. You're not thinking of giving that up for a girl, are you?"

I hadn't thought of it that way before.

Could I give up hockey?

"Come on, man. Tell me you're not fucking seriously thinking about this."

"I'm not. I just need her to open up to me. Mom and Dad always made this shit look easy. Now here I am with two kids, no wife, and a woman I think could be *the* woman. And I don't know, man . . . It doesn't feel right." Even saying the words out loud feels fucking wrong. I just don't know why. Or what the hell I'm missing.

"Okay. So if you ever tell anyone I said this, I swear to the fucking hockey gods, brother, I will deny, deny, deny, then kill you. You got me?"

I laugh at my idiot brother because what else can I do when he says shit like that?

"Mom and Dad *did* make it look easy. And I think that was half your problem with Helene. Seriously. You just wanted the family we had and figured it wouldn't be hard. You had the girl. You had the kid. You're Cross fucking Wilder. Everything has always come easy for you. Things just sort of fell into place for you. Then they didn't. And I really don't think you would have bothered walking away if Helene hadn't done it for you, just because it would have been easier to stay in a loveless relationship than walking away and finding someone to make you happy. You may have found her, but you've got a big old fucking problem. You like simple. You like easy. And Everly doesn't seem like either of those things."

"You don't know her," I grumble, not able to deny the rest of what he's saying. Even if I wish I could.

"I didn't say she wasn't worth it. I said she's not making it easy for you. You're not afraid of hard work, Cross. And I think this girl is going to make you work for it."

"You know you're an asshole, right?" I fucking mumble as we turn into the parking lot.

"What did I do?" Ares laughs because he knows he didn't do anything.

"You made sense."

Everly

I smile when I walk into the studio Saturday morning and find Bellamy and Kerrigan already there, talking with Gracie.

Grace is covering class this morning because I've got an

early cheer practice and her dance practice isn't until later this afternoon.

"Hey, little miss," I squat down in front of Kerrigan, and she throws her arms around my shoulders and squeezes.

"Miss Evie," she whispers, hanging on tight. I look up at Bellamy, whose got a sad smile on her face.

"She's missing Cross pretty bad, so we decided to go to breakfast before class today. Sorry we're a few minutes early."

"I understand." I pull back and smile at Kerrigan. "I'm missing your daddy too. But he comes home tonight."

"But I'll be sleeping by then," she pouts.

"You will," Bellamy agrees. "But we're going to have a princess movie marathon, remember? We're going to pop popcorn and eat cookies and watch all the movies until you fall asleep. Then when you wake up, Daddy will be home."

"That sounds like so much fun," I tell her as I stand and look around for Jax. "Where's the baby?"

"Mom stole him from Bellamy a few minutes ago. She's changing him in her office." Grace sips her water. "You may never get him back. Mom loves babies."

"Miss Evie . . ." Kerrigan tugs on my hoodie. "Do you want to watch princess movies wif us?"

"Oh, sweets," Bellamy looks at me like she's mortified. "Miss Evie probably has something—"

"I'd love to watch princess movies with you. How about I bring the cupcakes?"

"Wif strawberries?" Kerrigan asks excitedly.

"As long as Miss Amelia has them, I'll make sure we get them."

Bellamy's entire stance softens, and she mouths, *thank you.*

"Well what about me?" Gracie asks, and Kerrigan's eyes double in size. "Do you have room for one more?"

"I think we can make room," Bellamy tells her as Mom walks in from her office with a giggling Jax in her hands.

"There we go. All changed and happy, aren't we, handsome?" She blows a raspberry on his cheek, and he coos as he smacks her face.

"Hi, Mom." I move next to her and take Jax out of her hands. "Hey, little man. I missed you too." He immediately fists my hair and buries that face in my neck, and I just breathe him in while the girls all stare. "What? Jax and I had a heart-to-heart last week." I lean my head against his chubby little face. "We're buds, right?"

He tugs my hair again and giggles, and suddenly everything feels right.

More right than it's felt all week.

I turn back to Bellamy. "Any sweets requests for you?"

"Did someone say sweets?" Mom asks.

Grace shakes her head. "You two. How do you not both have a mouth full of cavities?"

"I always told you your good genetics came from me," Mom scolds. "Do you girls have plans tonight?"

I look down at Cross's shy little girl, smiling next to me. "We've got a date for a princess movie marathon."

"That sounds like fun. You know . . . if you like football, you could come to the game tomorrow. It's at home, and we have plenty of room in the suite. We haven't had babies in there for so long. It would be so much fun."

I'm not sure if my mom is talking to the three-year-old or her aunt, but they both look confused. "Our family has a private suite for the games," I tell Bellamy. "There's plenty of room if you'd like to come. Plus, apparently my mom is a great built-in babysitter."

"Will you be there?" Kerrigan asks with big hopeful eyes. Man, this kid could ask me for the moon, and I'd try to figure out a way to get it for her.

"I dance during the games. But Gracie will be there." Then I look back to Bellamy. "Caitlin comes sometimes too. She floats between our box and the Kingston's box."

"Thank you for the offer, Mrs. Sinclair. I'll let Cross know."

"Oh, honey, please call me Annabelle. And please let both of your brothers know. We'd love to have you all."

Okay. I might just kill my mom.

CINDERELLA

Hey, big man. Have a good game tonight.

CROSS

I heard a rumor you might be at my house when I get home. Any truth there?

CINDERELLA

Geez. Kerrigan sold me out? I guess three year olds can't keep secrets.

CROSS

You gonna stay after the movie?

CINDERELLA

Maybe.

CROSS

Be in my bed when I get home, Everly.

I gotta go.

I wipe the grease from Kerrigan's lips as she makes a mess of her pizza. "Daddy never lets us eat in front of the TV."

"What we don't tell Daddy won't hurt us." Bellamy links

her pinky with Kerrigan's, and I smile at Grace. We still link pinkies.

Caitlin came over too and brought a few of her old pageant crowns with her. So the four of us are sitting in front of Cross's giant flat-screen, watching *Tangled* in tiaras while we eat pizza and strawberry shortcake. Not a bad night.

By the time Kerrigan is asleep on the couch a few hours later, we've finished *Tangled* and moved on to *Frozen* and *Frozen 2*. For a little girl who doesn't talk very much, she sure does like to sing along with her movies, and it's adorable.

Kerrigan is sleeping with her head on my lap, and Jax is zonked-out, milk-drunk and tucked against my shoulder when Bellamy switches the TV over to the game. "Have you ever seen Cross play, Everly?"

I watch the man on the TV. Strong and smooth and skating so damn fast.

"No. Hockey's never been my thing." Total lie. I used to love going to Keith's hockey games when we were in college.

But as I watch Cross bank off the boards behind the net and score, it's hard for me not to cheer. If I didn't have both kids sleeping on me, I'd probably be jumping up and down.

"Oh my God," I gasp as a guy from the other team slams into him, and Cross flies backward into the metal goalpost. His helmet comes loose and off his head right before his skull hits the ice, and my heart stops.

Ares rips his gloves off and throws them to the ice right before he rails on the player who just hit Cross. The commentators are talking about the fight, but I can only see Cross not moving. "Bellamy," I croak out on a whisper.

She grabs my hand, and Gracie pulls her phone out. "I'll call Brynn."

"Wait." The word comes out short and curt, but I need to see Cross stand up.

He's going to stand up.

Brynlee and the other trainer move out onto the ice, and after a minute, Cross is up on his skates, being helped off. But I still don't think I can breathe. Holy shit.

---

*O*nce I help Bellamy put the kids to bed, I call Cross and leave him a voicemail. Then I also shoot him off a text, before leaving another message, but I don't hear back.

I try to blame that on the uneasy feeling I get when I make my way into his room with the overnight bag I packed. I feel like I'm invading his space. I've never been in here with him. I'm not sure I *want* to be in here without him either. Mind made up, I wash my face and thank my mom for those damn good genetics again because I don't mind being makeup-free. I change into black sleep shorts, white knee socks, a tank, and decide to steal one of Cross's Revolution hoodies because it smells like him.

Cute and still sexy, without being something I'd be ashamed to be seen wearing in front of Ares, because my ass is waiting for my man on the couch.

Not his bed. Not tonight.

When I get back downstairs, Bellamy is already on the couch. "Couldn't sleep," she offers. I'm pretty sure seeing Cross go down tonight bothered her too.

"Me neither."

She grabs the remote and turns the TV back on. "Want to watch the new season of *The Kings Of Kroydon Hills*? It dropped yesterday."

"Sure." I sit down and curl my feet under my body. "Did you know this is based on my aunt's novels? We all joke that it's really based on her and my uncle, but she swears it's not."

"Is your uncle as hot as the guy on the show?"

"Eww. I don't know."

We both turn when the door opens hours later and Cross walks in, wearing sunglasses with Ares behind him, carrying both bags. Bellamy runs over to her brother to fawn over him, while I stand frozen in place.

"I'm fine, B. Just hit the lights off for me for a few minutes."

He moves around her, slowly and a little unsteady, and takes two steps toward me before I walk straight into his chest and wrap my arms around his waist. "You scared me."

He buries his face in my hair and inhales. "Sorry. I didn't know you'd hear about it before I could tell you."

"I didn't hear about it, Cross. We were watching it. I called and texted. I was worried."

"Sorry, blondie. I've got his phone." Ares pulls the phone from his pocket and hands it to me. "Big brother has a moderate concussion and some blurred vision. He's not allowed any screen time yet. So no phone. But they want him to rest. No strenuous activity. No heavy concentrating. But they said he doesn't need complete darkness and quiet. So there's that. I'm sure you guys can come up with some less than strenuous activity."

I tuck his phone into the pocket of my hoodie. "I'm not sure if I like you yet, God of War."

"I have that effect on people." Ares looks at me funny. "You staying the night?"

"Yes." I fit myself under Cross's arm. "Come on, big man. Let's go to bed."

He groans, and the vibrations do funny things to my heart.

"Gotta say, didn't think I'd have to be concussed to get you in my bed, Cinderella."

Ares shakes his head and walks up the stairs ahead of us. "I'll drop your bag in your room."

"Thanks, man," Cross groans and grabs the banister, then makes his way slowly up the stairs. He stops to peek in on Kerrigan and Jax, then walks into the master bedroom at the back of the house and drops down on the bed.

Ares places Cross's bag in the corner and pulls me aside as Bellamy fills Cross in on the kids stuff from the weekend. "Listen, I know you don't like me. So you might not like what I'm about to say. But Cross really got his bell rung. The next few days are going to suck. His eyes are bothering him. His head's gonna hurt like a fucking bitch. And he's gonna be angry because he's off the ice for at least two weeks. If you can't handle that, leave now. Tell him you need to go home for something, and I'll make sure he's good."

"Well damn . . ."

Ares crosses his thick arms over his chest and waits.

"Maybe you do have a redeeming quality, after all. I've got a football game tomorrow, but I can skip it. I'll message Miss Cassabian and let her know someone needs to take my place."

"You don't have to do that. Bellamy and I will be here."

"Thanks, but I wasn't asking for your permission."

We stand, locked in a stare-off until his lips tip up in a cocky grin. "Don't fuck him over, blondie."

"Better men than you have underestimated me, God of War. They regret it now."

"What's going on over there?" Cross calls from his bed.

"I was just telling blondie, if she'll take care of you, Bellamy and I have the kids tonight and tomorrow morning. You need to sleep. Doc said rest is the most important thing."

Cross's siblings walk out, closing the door behind them, and my big man grumbles something about sleeping the whole flight home. "I don't feel like sleeping."

I move between his legs, and his hands skim up the backs of my bare thighs.

"Doc said you had to relax, right?" I ask as an idea comes to me.

EVERLY

"You're kidding me, right?" Cross asks, not liking my idea.

"Nope. Not kidding. You have the tub my dreams are made of. I'm going to fill it with warm water, turn the lights off in the bathroom so you can rest your eyes, and I want you to relax in a bath."

"Everly . . . girls take baths. Men don't take baths."

"Your tub is really big, Cross."

I take his hand and tug him up off the bed, then pull him behind me into his bathroom. "Now sit."

I try not to think about the fact that his ex probably picked out the tacky, fluffy stool that goes with the built-in makeup vanity in his bathroom as I push him down on it and turn on the water. When I spin around, he looks less than impressed. "Just trust me."

I walk out of the room and turn the lights back on in the bedroom to give us a warm glow in the bathroom. Just enough to be able to see without it bothering his eyes. When I walk back in, I kneel in front of him. "What are you doing?"

At least when I'm on my knees, he doesn't sound as grouchy.

Silly man...

"I'm undressing you, Wilder. You can't take a bath fully clothed." I slip his glasses off first and gently press my lips to the purple bruise blooming on the side of his face.

"I don't want to take a bath at all, baby."

Yup. Me on my knees and one single press of my lips and he's calling me *baby*.

This man has no idea what he does to me.

I ignore his grouchy answer and take off one shoe, then the other before I strip him very carefully until he's gloriously naked. Taking my time to trace each defined muscle in his back. His chest. His abs. His body is a work of art.

"It's not nice to tease a man when he's down, Cinderella."

"Oh, honey." I make a dramatic attempt to look down at his dick. "You're nowhere near down, and I never said you were going to be in the tub alone. I just said it was a really big tub, and I thought a bath could relax you."

He runs his hands under my hoodie. "Always so pretty in my clothes, baby. We're gonna have to revisit these socks when I feel better."

"We'll revisit anything you want, as long as you follow the doctor's orders and rest, Cross."

"And you'll help me rest?" he questions, more upbeat now.

"Doctor's orders." I turn the water off, then take his hands. "Be careful. You're not completely steady."

He slowly sinks down in the bath, hissing. "Jesus, woman. Are you trying to burn my skin off?"

"Oh, shush. I like the water hot." I throw my hair up on top of my head and pull his hoodie off.

Cross stops grumbling as soon as I start stripping. "Slower, Everly. I'm seeing two of you right now, and I want to enjoy it."

"Enjoy it while you can. Because the only way you're getting two of me is if you get Gracie too, and you're not the only one who doesn't share."

I grab two towels from the linen closet and lay them on the tacky little chair, then slowly sink down into the water until my back is resting against Cross's chest.

"Let your hair down, Everly. I fucking love your hair."

"It'll get all wet," I argue as I lather up a loofah I found in the closet.

His hand trails up my body, and I feel him physically relaxing behind me. His breathing slows and evens, and I want to keep us this relaxed.

His hand trails up my neck and into my hair.

"Fine." I pull it out, and Cross runs his fingers through it immediately.

"You were right. This is relaxing." He takes a kid's plastic cup off the shelf next to the tub and fills it with water, then dumps it over my hair.

"I'm supposed to be taking care of *you*, Cross."

He squirts baby shampoo into my hair and lathers it up and then dumps the cup again. I hum at the divine feel of his hands massaging my scalp.

"How do you feel?" I ask as I turn and cup his face in my hands as gently as I can. "Does it hurt?"

"Feels like somebody hit the side of my head with a two-by-four. I really am seeing double. Not that I think there's two of you in front of me, but you're not one solid thing right now, if that makes sense."

"Close your eyes, baby." He does as I ask, and I ghost my lips over his before pressing my legs to either side of his to straddle his lap. Pressing myself against him, covering his body with mine.

Wishing I could make it all better, but knowing somehow, I take away some of the pain.

Cross's cock presses against me, and any doubts I had of where this was going vanish with the steam floating off the water. "If you move, this stops."

"Everly . . ." His hand slips to the small of my back, holding me against him.

"Not a muscle, Cross, or I'll stop," I tease as I rub myself along the length of his cock.

"I don't think this was what Doc had in mind when he said to relax." Cross's voice is low and slow and tinged in pain. "But if you stop right now, you might actually kill me."

"We wouldn't want that now, would we?" I brush my lips over his and slide his cock inside me.

Gripping the edges of his giant clawfoot tub, I move impossibly slow. My hips rise and fall. My breasts move in front of Cross's face. And I'm pretty sure this ridiculously sexy man could make me come, just from looking at him. So intense. So much emotion. It's overwhelming and addicting all at once.

"You scared me tonight, Cross."

He groans and tightens his grip on my hips. "I'm sorry, baby."

"Don't do it again." I take his hands in mine and move them to my breasts. Needing to feel him strong and solid and here with me.

"I'm not gonna last tonight, Everly."

I lean forward and take his bottom lip between mine, then bite down. "Then come, Cross."

"Fuck . . ." He groans out as he comes, giving me that extra push I need for my orgasm to wash over me like a warm wave pulling me under. "Christ, Everly. I fucking love you."

My eyes fly to his, thinking I heard him wrong, because there's no way he just said he loved me, but Cross's eyes are closed as he leans back in the tub. Utterly relaxed.

Ummm . . . He may be relaxed now, but I think I'm about to have a nervous breakdown.

Cross

I wake up the next morning to a dark room, an empty bed, and cold sheets.

Shit.

She bolted.

I'm a fucking asshole. And now I'm a pissed-off asshole. She didn't even talk to me.

I swing my legs over the bed and immediately regret the fast movement when the room spins around me and my stomach threatens to revolt if I don't slow it the fuck down.

I knew it was a mistake as soon as the words left my mouth last night. Not that I don't love Everly—because I fucking do. But because she's not ready to hear it.

I grab my sweats from the foot of the bed, and this time when I stand, I take it slower. My vision still isn't at 100 percent and this shit's going to drive me crazy. It's been years since my last concussion, but that one only gave me migraines for a few weeks. My vision was fine. This is annoying as fuck.

I walk by Kerrigan's empty bedroom, then stop and stare into Jax's nursery. Everly's sitting in the glider, giving Jax a bottle. She's back in those tiny shorts that barely cover her ass, those white socks are pulled up to her knees, and my hoodie is dwarfing her body. And she's singing to my son while he plays with her hair.

My vision might be fucked, but the sight of her takes my breath away.

Jax finishes his bottle, and she pops him on her shoulder to burp while smiling at me. "Good morning, Cross."

Then Jax burps right away and squeals when Everly stands, and he catches his first glimpse of me. Man, being away from my kids fucking blows.

I move into the room and wipe his face. "Hey, little man. Daddy missed you."

"We were trying to let you sleep." She moves over to the changing table and gets Jax cleaned up and dressed for the day like a pro. "Kerrigan is downstairs. Bellamy and she are making waffles, I think."

I reach out and grab her arm. "Hey, slow down."

She stops and looks up at me through her lashes. "Brynn called. She's stopping by this afternoon to check on you. You may have to see a specialist in the city tomorrow."

"We have to talk, Everly."

My stomach sinks when she walks by me. "Later, Cross."

"Don't you have a game today?"

"I'm going to call and let them know I can't make it."

Shit. "Don't you fucking dare do that. I'm fine."

I'm also full of shit. I'm not fine. Even raising my voice that little bit hurts my head.

"Excuse me?" Her words drip with anger, and apparently my brain really isn't working because I just keep saying the wrong thing.

"You're a professional. You can't miss a game because I have a concussion. There's nothing you can do here. I don't need anyone's help." Shit. It's like I can't stop the bullshit spewing from my lips. "Go to the game. You can always come back after."

"Oh I can, can I?" She looks from Jax to me, and for a second, I think she might cry. "This is why I don't date athletes. You're all big fucking babies."

"Hey, blondie. Waffles are ready," Ares calls out as he

comes to a stop in front of Jax's door. "He wakes. How are you feeling, man?"

"He does," Everly snaps at Ares. "And he's in a lousy fucking mood." She gently hands Jax to him, then kisses Jax's cheek. "He's been fed and changed. Now it's your turn to deal with the bigger baby in the room." And when she storms out, Ares turns to me, looking like he's enjoying my pain.

"Dude. What the fuck did you do? I figured a concussion was a Get-Out-of-Jail-Free card."

When I don't answer, the fucker laughs. "Did you call her the wrong name or something?"

"Yeah, or something."

Because what I did was somehow worse.

I sit on the couch a few hours later, with Brynlee sitting across from me, and Everly and Ares standing next to her, like two of the four horsemen of the fucking apocalypse. Everly hasn't said a word to me since this morning, but she's hanging on every word Brynn says. "We've already scheduled an appointment with a specialist in the city, Cross. It's tomorrow at two. Can someone take you? You can't drive yet."

"I will," Everly tells Brynlee. *Not me.*

Nope. She's not even looking at me.

"Thanks, blondie. I've got practice, and Bellamy's got school. Mrs. A will have the kids."

"You guys *do* know I'm sitting right here, right?" I ask while they all make schedules for me without talking to me. Like I'm not right here.

"We got this, Cross. You're good," Ares tells me, like

suddenly he's the adult in the room. It's fucking weird and makes my head hurt worse.

"How long am I off the ice, Brynn?" I ask, needing to get back out there.

"I'm going to take a rough guess that it should be at least ten days. Maybe two weeks. I want to know what they say tomorrow. We'll have a better feel after that. I don't like that you're vision is still wonky, Cross. That concerns me."

"Is wonky your official diagnosis, Brynn?" Ares asks in a flirty tone.

Everly smacks his chest. "Back off, God of War. Keep your flirting away from my roommates."

"Dude. You wound me," he scoffs.

"I will wound you if you screw my friends," she tells him with a teasing smile.

What the hell? She's smiling at him?

"When did you two start getting along? How long was I out?" I ask, and they both look at me like I'm crazy.

"I want you to rest, Cross. It's the most important thing. Sleep. Let your body heal." Brynn closes her bag and stands. "You coming home tonight, Evie?"

"That's up for debate," she tells her, then looks over at me. "We'll see if he keeps saying stupid things."

Brynlee holds back a smile. "In his defense, his brain was basically scrambled like an egg last night. Give it a few more days. I brought you a bag of your things, just in case. Your sketchbook, some clothes. You know, the necessities."

Everly hugs Brynlee. "Thanks, Brynn. I appreciate it. You going to the game?"

"Yeah. I'm heading there now." Brynn looks over at me. "No TV, Cross. Not even a Kings game. Rest."

"Thanks for coming, Brynn."

Ares walks Brynlee out, and I close my eyes, tired of trying to stop the spinning room.

THE WILDCAT

Soft fingers run gently over my forehead. "You need to lie down, Cross. Why don't you go to bed for a little while? Take a nap."

I grab her wrist and bring her palm to my lips. "I'm sorry for what I said this morning. I just hated the idea of you missing your game for me."

"Listen to me, Cross Wilder, because I'm only going to say this once. I've been dancing every single day of my life since I could walk. I've been cheering professionally since I turned eighteen. That's five years already. That's two more than the average professional cheerleader. I wasn't even sure I wanted to do it this year. But I love it, so I figured *why not*. Well, my why not came today. Skipping was an easy decision. You're an easy why not. You're hurt. You need help, whether your grouchy ass wants to admit it or not. You have two kids, who already missed you and weren't going to understand why Daddy doesn't feel good. A sister who's been filling in every night after the nanny left. And I may have underestimated Ares's ability to help, so I called out today without second-guessing it or regretting it. I didn't need your permission to do it. And I didn't appreciate you making me feel stupid about choosing you over a football game either."

"You about done?" I ask quietly because my brain hurts.

Everly nods and puts her hands on her legging-covered hips.

Hips I want to feel curled against me while I sleep.

So fucking sexy.

The shorts are gone now, but she's still wearing my hoodie with my name across the back, and I fucking love it.

"I'm sorry. I woke up this morning, and you weren't there. I thought you left after last night. I felt like an asshole, and I feel like shit, and I lashed out at you. Make sure you understand what I'm saying here, Everly. Because I'm not sorry for what I said last night. I'm sorry I said it *then*. I know you're not ready to hear it, and I should have waited. I *am* sorry for the way I spoke to you this morning though. That was wrong. Now please fucking tell me I'm forgiven, so I can lie down and close my eyes without wondering if I'm going to lose you while I sleep."

"Can I join you?"

"Yeah, baby. Let's go lie down."

The Philly Press

KROYDON KRONICLES

WILDSIN

Cross Wilder was spotted again yesterday being chauffeured around town by our favorite blonde bombshell. It seems not even a concussion can dampen our newest #KroydonKouple romance. Do we think that twinkle in his eye could be love? One can only hope. Stay tuned for more, peeps!
#KroydonKronicles #WildSin

EVERLY

"They're so full of shit." I look up from my phone, where I've just read the most recent post by the Kroydon Kronicles, to where Lindy and Griffin sit across from me in Sweet Temptations. "They couldn't even see his damn eyes. He was wearing sunglasses because his eyes are still sensitive."

I stuff a giant piece of chocolate chip muffin in my mouth and ignore the looks Lindy is shooting my way. I know I look insane.

"Evie, if you get any more upset, you're going to go into a sugar coma," she warns me very cautiously, like she's approaching a wild animal, who's equally as likely to break down and cry as she is to attack the people sitting across from her.

That's me. I'm the wild animal.

"He's driving me crazy. He's the worst patient I've ever seen. And that's saying something because my dad was pretty bad a few years ago when he messed up his knee. Cross is worse."

Gracie sits down and passes out our coffees. "Really? Dad

was pretty bad. I'm not sure I believe anyone could be worse than that."

"He doesn't want me to do anything for him. And he told me if I didn't go to work today, he was going to drive me here himself," I groan.

"So what did you do?" Lindy asks as she takes the lid off her coffee and inhales deeply. "When you guys have kids, don't breastfeed. I limit myself to one coffee a day, and I swear I'd savor it for two hours if I had the patience, just to make it last longer."

"Ok-ay," Gracie laughs. "But seriously, Evie. What *did* you do? You don't even work today."

"I hid his keys, made Mrs. Ashburn promise she wouldn't tell him where they were, and called you guys for coffee. There's some stuff I can work on for the fashion show this weekend anyway. I'm going to stop into Le Désir after this. You're both still good for your fittings, right? Brynn and Kenzie have already had theirs."

"Remind me how I let you talk me into this?" Lindy smells her coffee again before finally taking the first heavenly sip and exhaling like she just tasted her salvation.

"You're an Olympic gold medalist with a world class body. And you're wearing boy-cut panties made of black lace with Swarovski crystals and your husband's hockey jersey. You're going to look stunning. That's how."

"I blame pregnancy brain. My stomach still isn't back to prebaby. I can't even see my abs," she whines.

"Your jersey will cover your stomach. You're going to look incredible," I tell her with complete confidence.

"Fine. What's *she* wearing?" Lindy groans and watches Gracie sip her decaf tea. "Seriously, Grace. What's the point of decaf?"

"I don't want to be jittery." Grace shrugs, like it's normal to not like coffee.

Sometimes, I wonder how we can be twins.

"She's wearing pink lace bikinis, with duchess satin ribbon ties at her hips, along with a white men's tank top with the Kings logo in pink crystals and Dad's name and number on the back." I sit up a little straighter because the design is so incredibly perfect and it's also perfectly Grace.

"Still thinking Dad's not going to be thrilled about that," Grace adds before she rips the tiniest chocolate chip out of my muffing and pops it into her mouth.

"Wait till he sees you're not wearing a bra," I tell her, then back away when she tries to hit me.

"Have you decided what you're wearing, Evie?" Gracie knows I haven't, but I guess that's what I get for refusing to let her wear a bra.

"Not yet." I look away, knowing I need to decide soon.

"Clock's ticking, Sinclair." Lindy sips her coffee and smiles like the Mad Hatter. "And it would be nice to know my husband isn't the only one who's going to be spanking an ass that night."

Gracie blows out a long breath. "I really wish someone would spank *my* ass."

"I volunteer as tribute," comes from an obnoxiously loud male voice.

We all turn around to find Maddox and his and Lindy's cousin, Maverick, walking toward us.

"Sorry," Grace dismisses Mav's offer. "I should have been more specific. I really wish I could find a *man* to spank my ass."

Maddox gags, and Maverick's smile grows. "Like I said—"

"Call me when you're old enough to buy a beer, Mav." Gracie shakes her head.

"Don't give him false hope, Grace." I stand and grab my bag. "I've got to go. I'll see you guys in the shop tomorrow for your fittings. Don't forget."

I spend the next few hours working on last-minute preparations for the weekend, then contemplate swinging by the condo for a change of clothes but decide against it. When I get back to Cross's that night, he's in Jaxon's favorite spot, swaying on the hammock. Both have their eyes closed, with Cross's leg hanging down to the ground so he can keep the motion going.

"Hey," I murmur, not wanting to wake Jax. I fix his blanket and run my fingers along Cross's arm. "How are you feeling?"

Cross cracks an eye open. "Not bad. I talked to Doc and Brynn today. I'm out for at least another week."

"I'm sorry, Cross. I know that's not what you wanted to hear." I run the backs of my fingers along his face. "Can I get you anything?"

"Nothing I can't get myself." His words are soft and probably not meant to sting, but that doesn't stop the bite.

"Okay. Well, I'm going to get my bag. I'm going back to my condo tonight after cheer practice."

"You finally running, Everly?"

"Nope. But I don't live here, Cross. And if you don't need my help, then I'm just somebody warming your bed." I kiss his forehead and step back. "I'm not running. I'm going home."

"Everly . . ." he groans my name, and Jax whimpers.

"I'll call you after cheerleading tonight."

It's only been a handful of days but walking away feels wrong.

"You leaving already, blondie? You just got here." Ares shuts the fridge and offers me a water.

I shake my head. "I've got cheer tonight, then I'm going home."

"You are home." He smirks, but I don't.

"Sorry, Ares. He's all yours tonight. This isn't my home. These aren't my kids. And Cross Wilder isn't my husband. If he doesn't want me here to help him, there's no reason for me to stay. I might be unsure of a lot of things, but I damn sure know better than to fall into a relationship of convenience. If he wants me here, he needs to use his damn words and tell me, instead of basically telling me to leave, which is what he's done for days now."

"I warned you he'd be an ass."

"Yup. And I'm not walking away. I'm just going to practice and to sleep in my own bed. See you later, God of War."

If I don't think about it too hard, maybe I'll actually believe my own words.

Cross

Ares waits for Everly to leave before he turns around and looks at me.

He could see me the whole time she was basically calling me out for being a dick.

"You done fucked up this time, brother."

"And you wonder why I say you've taken too many hits to the head." I buckle Jax into his high chair and sprinkle a few puffy snack things on his tray, then glare at my brother. "You wouldn't fucking understand."

"Try me."

"It's been a fucked up week. I already missed one game. I'm missing another one tomorrow. It looks like I'm going to miss the first game of the season. I'm fucking pissed. And every time I open my mouth with Everly, the wrong thing comes out. She wants to wait on me, and that's the last fucking thing I want. She's not supposed to be taking care of me. *I'm* supposed to take care of her. That's how this works."

"Bullshit." Bellamy walks into the kitchen with her hands planted on her hips and such a pissed-off expression on her face, I should probably be scared. "Jesus. Do you even hear yourself?"

When I don't say anything, she moves past me and pulls the food Mrs. Ashburn left for us out of the refrigerator, then turns on the oven. "Do you think Mom never took care of Dad?"

When Ares and I don't answer, she makes a noise somewhere between a shriek and a groan, and Jax laughs at her. "Don't be a dick like your daddy and uncle when you grow up, Jaxon."

"Hey—" I start, and she puts her hand up.

"Just stop, Cross. You've been a bear all week. *All. Week.* And Everly has done nothing but take it. She's helped with the kids. With you. With anything you needed, and you've been mean. And now you're saying it's basically because your ego is bruised. Grow up."

"My ego? What the hell, Bellamy?"

She pops the chicken in the oven, then crosses her arms over her chest, ready to spit fire. "Did Helene ever do anything for you? Hmm?"

"She's got nothing—"

"Answer the damn question, Cross," my sister demands.

The sad thing is I can barely even remember a time she took care of Kerrigan. "Helene never did anything that wasn't for Helene. Why?"

"Because somehow, you've gotten it in your head that you're supposed to be the one who does everything. That's not how relationships work. You're supposed to do things for each other. Let her take care of you, Cross. Don't push her away because she's a strong equal and not a damsel in distress."

"I'm not," I argue.

Ares moves next to Bellamy, like they're working together for an intervention. "You are, brother. Even I can see that."

"Well fuck," I groan.

"Might be grand gesture time, man."

I look between the two of them. "I can't believe I'm about to say this. What do you think I should do?"

"The fashion show is this weekend." Bellamy grabs an envelope off the counter. "Everly left tickets for all of us."

Fuck. I forgot that was this weekend.

Bellamy hands me the envelope but doesn't let go. "You think your head will be okay in a roomful of people?"

"Guess we're going to find out."

CROSS

> I'm sorry I'm an asshole, and I'm sorry I can't seem to stop.

CINDERELLA

> I kinda like that you're the one giving me whiplash for a change. It's nice not to be the one in the wrong for once.

CROSS

> You still staying at your place tonight?

CINDERELLA

Yeah. Practice sucked and I've got to be at the shop early tomorrow. Then practice again tomorrow night. Saturday is the fashion show and Sunday is a home game. It's going to be a crazy few days.

CROSS

Okay. I'll see you soon, Cinderella.

CINDERELLA

See you soon, Cross.

Guess she didn't believe me when I said I'd chase her. Her mistake.

The Philly Press

KROYDON KRONICLES

LIGHTS, CAMERA, FASHION!

Who else is living for the big Le Désir fashion show tonight? The glitz. The glam. The beautiful women in beautiful lingerie. Rumor has it we should get more than one *Kroydon Kouple* sighting too, considering Madeline Kingston-Hayes and Everly Sinclair are both walking in the show. Guess we're on #Hazey and #WildSin watch. Check back tomorrow for all the deets!
#KroydonKronicles

EVERLY

"Has anybody seen Lilah?" Carys yells with straight pins clamped tightly between her teeth before my cousin rushes into the room.

"I'm here. I'm here. Sorry." Lilah looks around with wild eyes. I haven't seen her in months since she's been on the US leg of her tour.

"Come with me," I pull her behind me and grab the heels to go with her lingerie. Lilah's wearing an ice-blue babydoll with a built-in pushup bra and white lace trim along with a matching floor-length robe.

It's gorgeous, if I do say so myself, which I do.

With her golden skin and nearly white-blonde hair, she looks innocent and pure. Angelic. Not at all the hell-raiser she's been her whole life.

I grab her white-satin mule heels, covered in white fuzzy feather tips on the strap crossing her toes, and I add a double-sided sticky pad to the inside sole of each heel. "Slide these on and let me see the whole thing."

She does as she's told, then spins.

"You look absolutely perfect, little cousin." Okay, so I may preen a little. Carys and Chloe let me design her lingerie.

She pulls at the sash on the robe I'm wearing. "Now let me see what you've got under there, Evie. I heard you designed mine, yours, and Gracie's. Come on, show me."

Gracie joins us in our little corner of the craziness backstage.

"Oh my God, Gracie . . ." Lilah squeals and walks in a circle around Grace. "Holy shit. You look so fucking hot. If I had your tits, I'd never wear a bra."

The three of us break out into a fit of laughter, like we do whenever we're all together.

"Lilah Belle—"

"Oh shit. Middle-named." Lilah giggles and turns to see Aunt Nattie and Mom standing behind us.

"Did you not think to stop home and see your father and me before you came here?" Nattie looks pissed. "We haven't seen you in a month."

Aunt Nat and Uncle Brady fly out to Lilah's shows whenever they can, but their youngest is still in school, so it's not like they can be there constantly.

"Sorry, Momma. Noah and I crashed as soon as we landed. It was stupid early. And I guess jet lag messed with us worse than we thought because I swear I almost overslept and missed this."

"Oh. My. God. I would have killed you," Carys shrieks as she joins us. "My girls all together. Just missing a few." She clears her throat. "Everly . . . there's someone here to see you."

She steps aside, and there he is.

My tall, dark, and handsome man.

"Is that him?" Aunt Nat asks Mom, who nods.

"Who's him?" Lilah murmurs. "And my goodness . . . does he have any brothers?"

"Yup," Gracie adds. "The God of War. But stay far away

THE WILDCAT

from that one."

"God of War?" Lilah parrots back.

"Don't ask," I tell her and slowly move to Cross. "Hi, handsome."

He reaches for me as soon as I'm within arm's reach and drags me against him. "You look beautiful, baby."

"He called her baby," Aunt Nattie snickers.

Mom laughs. "Yes, he did."

"He can call *me* baby," Lilah tells them both, and I smile at Cross.

"You know my whole family is here tonight, right?"

He looks behind me. "Is that them?"

"Ha. He wishes," Nattie answers for me.

I take his hand and pull him toward them. "Nat, Lilah, this is Cross. Cross, this is my aunt and cousin."

"Oh, this is going to be so much fun," Nattie smiles so damn big, she looks like she's about to swallow her face.

"Okay, you've met. Now, can I have a few minutes before this starts, please?" I ask the peanut gallery.

Carys looks at the time. "Ten minutes, Everly. Not a second more."

"Thanks." I link my hands with Cross and pull him out of the room and off to the side of the stage, so I can peek around the thick purple curtain. "Wow. The place is packed."

"Yeah. This place is really something." He's not wrong. The top floor of this hotel has a domed-glass ceiling, and we lucked out with a beautiful crystal-clear sky tonight. Not that I would have minded the rain.

The lighting in in here is amazing, and the vibes are so cool and trendy.

It's perfect for Chloe and Carys and all the designs.

Cross lifts his hands to touch my hair, and I take a step back. "Uh-uh. No touching anything, Wilder. This took hours to do."

Cross settles for fingering the red bow placed perfectly on top of my high ponytail.

"You gonna let me see what's under that robe?" he growls, and for a second, I feel like I got my Cross back.

"Nope. Not yet. You've got to wait to see like everyone else." I lean in quickly and give him the tiniest peck, then wipe the bright-red lip gloss from his lips. "How are you feeling?"

"Better," he grunts. "My eyesight is still fucked. I'm not seeing two of you anymore. But it's still hard to focus."

"I missed you."

His face softens. "Then why did you stay away?"

"Because I had work and practice and needed to get ready for this. And you didn't want me there, Cross. I'm a flight risk when I know I'm wanted. Tell me enough that you don't want my help, and I go from flight risk to gone in a heartbeat. And you didn't want my help." I run my thumb over his bottom lip. "How are the babies?"

"Kerrigan was upset because Grace taught her class this morning. She wanted to know where you were."

Well, damn. That hits hard. "I had cheer practice."

"She wants to watch you cheer. So does her dad."

My stomach somersaults. "I guess it's a good thing my family has a big box then, isn't it?"

"Yeah, baby. I guess it is."

Gracie moves in behind Cross and gives me *the get your butt moving* look.

"I've got to go." I take a step back as Cross wraps a hand around the back of my hair and pulls me in for a kiss that makes my toes curl.

"Yeah, babe. You better go fix that lipstick."

"Cocky fucker," I tease.

"Arrogance, baby. That's arrogance."

Cross

$\mathcal{I}$ watch her walk away before her mom and aunt each link their arms through mine. "Come on, Cross. Let's buy you a drink," the aunt says. I think her name is Nattie.

"He can't drink, Nat. He's got a concussion," Annabelle tells her as they lead me back to a bar with a group of people. Some I've met, others I haven't. But one I can pick out in a crowd. "Declan," his wife calls out to him, and Declan Sinclair, the best quarterback to ever play the game, turns around.

Yeah. He's also the father of the woman I'm fucking in love with.

And he may or may not be looking at me like he's going to need help burying my body later.

"Declan, honey, this is Cross." Annabelle drops my arm, and I reach my hand out to him.

"Nice to meet you, sir." Fuck. *Sir?* Really? Thirty-one goddamned years old, and I'm calling him sir.

Everyone around us stops and stares. "You know my best friend is Sam Beneventi."

"Who?" I ask, genuinely having no clue who that is when everyone breaks out laughing.

"Don't fuck over my daughter, and you'll never need to worry about it." Declan shakes my hand, and I see a guy around the same age as him shaking his head.

"Smooth, Dec. Just use me as your muscle." Guess he's Sam.

The owner of Sweet Temptations wraps an arm around

his waist. "You're still big and scary, honey. It's okay."

Easton Hayes steps beside me. "I warned you they were crazy. It started with their parents."

"Want to fill me in on the secret?" I ask him as Ares moves in next to me, and Maddox slides in on the other side of Easton.

"Nah," Maddox says. "It's more fun this way."

"You ready for this, E man?" Callen asks as he hands out beers to everyone but me. "Sorry to hear about the concussion. Fucking sucks."

"Thanks," I grumble, not really used to hanging out with a group of guys I don't know well.

"Fuck no. I'm not ready. My wife is going to walk a runway in her underwear. I don't know how I'm supposed to be okay with that."

Maddox slaps his back. "Because you're who she's going home with. Besides, I think half the men in this room are related to Lindy. Nobody's looking at her like that. Now, this guy," he tilts his head toward me. "You're fucked, dude. Most of the guys in this room want to nail your girl. Especially when they realize they're two of them."

Ares laughs, and I feel my head start to throb. "Thanks, asshole. That's just the thought I needed."

"You're welcome. That's for banging her in my office."

I laugh for the first time in a week. "Yeah. Okay. I deserve that."

"Seriously. I've been kicking guys' asses for years, defending the two of them," Callen adds.

I want to ask if they know who hurt my girl because somebody did.

But it's not their place to tell me if they *do* know.

That has to come from her.

"Yeah," Maddox agrees. "Trouble didn't date."

"Trouble?" I ask, trying to follow along.

"It's what Maddox calls Lindy," Easton explains.

"Yeah. She didn't date," Maddox adds, and Easton's chest puffs up like a peacock. "And Brynn's dad is a former heavyweight MMA champion, so nobody was willing to go near her. And Kenzie was always more interested in school than guys. But fucking A. The twins. The twins had to beat guys away with a fucking stick their whole lives."

Callen nods. "More like *we* did. Every asshole with eyes hit on them."

"Yeah. Have fun with that. We're officially passing the baton. They're yours." Maddox grins, and it's a little fucking creepy.

"Only one of them is mine," I say with a smile. Because she really is.

"Nope. They're a package deal." Callen wraps an arm around me and walks me to a front row seat next to Everly's family. "Good luck, dude."

The lights blink, and the curtain opens after a minute to a band on the platform at the back of the t-shaped stage. Everly's cousin Lilah comes out with a microphone in hand. "Hey, everyone. I'm Lilah Ryan, and I'm so excited to be here tonight, celebrating my incredible aunts and their beautiful lingerie."

A light beat is ticked off on the drums before the tiny blonde starts humming along and opens her mouth.

Holy. Shit.

That voice.

That's when it clicks.

That's Lilah Ryan.

The Lilah Ryan who's been touring the country and is on every radio station and every Instagram reel you hear. That's Everly's cousin.

Lilah sings in the center of the catwalk as models strut up and down for a solid twenty minutes. Some are dressed in sexy pajamas. Little nighties. Sheer robes. Every bra and underwear combo I could have ever imagined.

Once Lilah announces the last song and Kenzie walks out, I hold my fucking breath.

She goes first, wearing a vintage black Philadelphia Kings t-shirt tied in a knot above her stomach, along with black bikini bottoms.

Brynlee follows her in a dark-green Crucible gym muscle tee. A hot-pink bra peeks out of the big sleeve openings, and when she turns around to strut back, I'm not sure who groans louder, Ares or Callen, because my physical therapist's very fine ass is on full display in an emerald-green thong.

Callen doesn't sound happy.

Serves him right for torturing me.

Shithead.

Lindy comes up behind Lilah next, and Easton groans. She's wearing a shrunken Revolution jersey with navy-blue, sparkly boy-cut underwear. Definitely the most covered of the group. "Dude. Chill," Callen tells him. "She wears less than that on the beach."

"Fuck off, Sinclair."

I bite back my laugh because even from here, I can see Gracie coming next, which means Everly is last. Grace has pink panties and a tight, white, ribbed Kings tank top with Sinclair and the number thirteen written in some kind of pink glitter on the back. You'd think since she looks just like Everly, I'd like seeing her half naked, but it does nothing for me. Even before I see Everly step foot on stage and high-five her cousin as she passes her, I feel her.

Holy. Fucking. Hell.

Her golden hair sits high on her head in a ponytail, falling in big curls down her back. Dramatic makeup makes her aqua eyes pop, and those pouty lips are painted cherry red.

And damn, if they don't match the tiny, cropped red Revolution tee she's wearing. With short little sleeves, it's cropped just under her chest, so I can see the bottom of her boobs bouncing with each step she takes in her red-soled heels. From the front, her red panties look like plain lace and silk. But when she gets to the end of the runway, I fight not to make a sound. Which is good because Everly's dad is seated a few seats down from me, and he's making enough comments for all of us. Poor guy.

Her panties barely cover her ass. Just the very top is covered in little red ruffles.

And her tiny t-shirt isn't blank.

No. That Revolution shirt is mine.

With my name and number on it.

She's wearing my name.

"Holy shit, brother. I think you just got claimed." Ares fucking laughs next to me.

And I'll be damned. I think he's right.

She might not want to go to one of my games, but that girl just told the whole fucking world she's mine.

I stand up, and Ares grabs my arm. "Where are you going?"

"To go get what's mine," I tell him, then stop in front of Declan Sinclair. "I'm in love with your daughter, sir."

Declan looks at me like I'm out of my fucking mind, and I might be.

"You look like you're ten years younger than me, Cross. Don't fucking call me *sir*. But go back there and tell my goddamned daughters to put on some clothes before I stroke out. And be at the game tomorrow and at my house afterward for dinner."

Annabelle smiles and lays her head on her husband's shoulder, like I just made her happy, which is good. Because Everly's probably going to kill me for this.

EVERLY

Carys and Chloe pop champagne backstage as we all celebrate a successful show. Everything went the way we planned, and it feels so good. Gracie throws her arms around me.

"I'm so proud of you, sissy." She squeezes so tightly I can barely breathe. "You helped do this. We're wearing your designs. You did it."

"I know. I can't even believe it," I tell her, still amazed I actually designed some of tonight's show.

"It's time, Everly. You need to do this for yourself. You've got your first line already done. You know you do. You've been working on it since your senior year." Gracie grabs Lindy, Kenzie, and Brynlee, and we all stand in the same circle we've been making since we played soccer together as little girls. "We've talked about it, and if you really don't want to use your trust fund, we'll all back you."

My heart skips a beat, and I stare at my friends on the verge of tears. "I love you guys. And you're right. It's time to do this for myself. I appreciate you offering to back me, but I've got the trust, and I need to do this on my own."

THE WILDCAT

"Can I work for you?" Lindy smiles over tears. "I'll do your marketing."

"Oh my goodness, Lindy. You're crazy. But I love you." I hug her and laugh.

"You think I'm kidding—"

"Oh shit," Brynn interrupts her, and I turn around just in time to see Cross walk into the room, looking like a man on a mission. Easton isn't far behind, but I only have eyes for my big guy. Which is good because before I take my next breath, he picks me up, throws me over his shoulder, and smacks my ass so hard I might actually come, hanging off him like this.

"Put me down, Cross. You have a concussion."

He smacks my ass again, and there's no way I don't have a bright-red handprint on my ass to match my bright-red panties. "A concussion, babe. I'm not dead. Now, where's a room with a lock on the damn door?" he growls, and I point him to the bathroom the models were using earlier.

"Oh my God, Cross." I laugh as his hand caresses my bare asscheek, and kicks the door shut behind me before he tries to figure out how to lock it. Once he's satisfied, he walks us into the room and sits me down on the vanity. "Fucking hell, Everly . . . You're wearing my name on your back."

"I am," I whisper back and stare blindly into his burning eyes, the look so unfamiliar and yet entirely intoxicating. "Are you upset?"

"No, baby." Cross runs his hands up my thighs, and his fingers dig in to the globes of my ass. "Why would I be mad at my woman wearing my name and number? Christ, Everly, I want to fuck you so bad."

His words do the most magically dirty things to my entire body. I wrap my legs around his waist and grab his belt. "So do it, Cross."

There's a heavy knock at the door. "Some of us have to actually use the bathroom, Everly."

"Oh my God." I drop my head to his. "How fast can you be?"

"Everly . . ." Another voice yells, and I'm pretty sure that one is Brynn. *Damn it.*

"Oh, I'm not gonna be fast tonight, baby. I'm going to fuck you for fucking hours." He pushes his tongue inside my mouth, and I press myself against him. "I'm going to take my time. Take your mouth and your cunt, and if you're a really good girl, I'm going to take this ass that you showed the whole world tonight."

"Yes, please." I vibrate with anticipation.

"Did you drive?" Cross pulls away, and it's as if the sun stopped shining and I'm desperate for its warmth. I nod my head. "Good. Let's go. I came here with Bellamy and Ares, but you and I are leaving alone. Grab your bag."

"But my family—"

"We'll see them all tomorrow after the game when we go to dinner at your parents' house," he tells me, and I stare at him, wondering if I'm in some kind of twilight zone. A second ago, he was filling every hole I had with his thick dick, and now we're having dinner with my crazy family.

"I'm sorry, what?" I hop off the counter. "Like my whole family?"

My voice actually cracks with that news. "I don't know if that's a good idea."

"Yeah well, your dad and I talked. I'm bringing the kids to the game tomorrow, and then we're all going to your parents' house for dinner. Now grab your stuff, and let's get the fuck out of here." Cross moves closer, his hand sliding down my back as he cups my ass. "And Everly . . . leave on the shirt."

We ride back to the house, bathed in silence, only talking enough to find out that Ares and Bellamy are still at the fashion show and Mrs. Ashburn is home with the kids. Cross holds my hand tucked in his like he's scared to let go.

Scared to let me go.

It doesn't take long to get to his house. And I can only imagine what it looks like when Mrs. Ashburn sees us walk in. "You're home early, Cross." She looks over at me and tries to hold her smile. "And don't you look ... pretty, Everly."

I probably look more like a high-end escort who went a little too heavy on the eye makeup and puffy hair. But I'll take pretty if it will get her out of here faster. The kids are asleep, and by the time Cross gets back inside from walking Mrs. A to her car, I've stripped down to my tee and panties.

He shuts and locks the door, then prowls toward me like an apex predator stalking its prey.

He knows I'm his. It's just a matter of how he wants to take me.

I turn around and lift my ponytail off my back. "I wasn't sure if you were going to like this, Wilder."

"Then you don't know fuck all about me, Sinclair. Because what you did tonight ... Damn, woman." He presses his lips to the base of the back of my neck and wraps my hair around his fist. "I thought I'd be the one to claim you in front of everyone, and even then, I figured it would scare the shit out of you." He pulls my hair out of the tie and lets it spill around my shoulders as he tilts my head back. "I never figured you'd do it first. But then, you like to keep me on my toes, don't you, baby?"

"I guess I do."

Strong hands wrap around my stomach and slide up my chest to cup my breasts, and Cross slides down my body.

"Fuck, baby. I can't believe you wore this onstage." He molds his big hands around the curves of my body, then slides his fingers along the hem of my panties, leaving delicious sparks of heat everywhere he touches.

"This ass . . ." He kisses one exposed cheek, then the other. "This body, draped in my name and my number . . ." A finger slides under the Brazilian-cut elastic sitting high on my backside and snaps it against my skin. "Why'd you do it?"

"Cross . . ." I whimper impatiently. "You want me to think with your face so close to my pussy?"

"If you want my tongue inside that sweet cunt, you're going to answer me, Everly."

"*Oh hell.* Because you're mine, Cross. You're mine, and I'm yours, remember?"

"Good girl." He bends me over the couch and smacks my ass. "Knew it would look so pretty covered in my handprint."

"Please, please, please," I beg.

He slides my panties to the side as his long, blunt finger moves through my wet sex. "Tell me you want this, Everly. Tell me you want everything I'm going to do to you. All of it."

"Cross . . ." The word is a plea mixed with a cry. "Don't make me think with you so close to giving us what we both need."

"Tell me, Everly," he demands in the sexiest voice I've ever heard, and I melt like warm ice cream on a scorching hot summer day.

"Do you want to know what scared me most this week?" I ask. He wanted honesty, I guess it's time to give it to him.

"I want to know everything, Everly." There's so much heartfelt emotion in his words, they strip me bare.

I look over my shoulder at this man kneeling behind me. Guess it's now or never. "The night you told me you loved me—"

"I already apologized for saying it then," he cuts me off, and I straighten and turn to face him.

"Listen to me, big man. Let me finish. It wasn't that you said it." He quirks his lips, and I cover them with my finger. "Okay, at first, it was that you said it. But then . . . then it was that I realized I wasn't scared of what you said. I was scared because I felt that way too. And I didn't know what to do with that."

Cross rocks back on his heels, then stands up in front of me. Towering over me.

"You're everything I was avoiding, Cross." I fist my hand in the front of his shirt and hold him in place, anchoring myself to him at the same time. "You're serious. A father with a family. You wanted a relationship. A commitment. You're an athlete and not just any athlete. You're a professional hockey player. If someone asked me to paint a picture of the man I didn't want to date, I would have painted you."

"Baby, I'm not sure how much more of this my ego can take." He runs his hand over my hair and holds my neck, locking us in place.

"But here's the thing. None of it mattered. Not what I thought I wanted. Or assumed I needed. Not why I felt that way. None of it mattered once you walked into my life. Because suddenly, it didn't matter what I believed. There was just you, and you didn't play by my rules."

"I was never playing a game."

"I know that now . . ." I stare into his dark eyes for a few long beats of my heart. "I'm not sure when I figured that out, but in my heart, I think I might have always known it. You still scare me, Cross, but I'm so damn in love with you, nothing else matters."

"That's good, baby. Because I wasn't letting you go."

Cross's big hands move to my hips, and he drops to his knees in front of me. "Have I told you how much I like these?" His lips kiss just above the edge of the silk, and I bury my hands in his thick hair. "Any chance you can wear this outfit for me after every game?"

"If you don't put your mouth on me soon, I may never wear them again."

Strong hands dig into my ass, tugging me forward until I stumble into him and grab his shoulders for balance. Cross buries his face in the gusset of my panties and inhales. "You smell delicious, Everly. Are you wet for me?"

"I'm soaked, Cross. I'm dripping for you. Are you going to make good on your promise and give me your mouth?"

"You're fucking right I am." He boosts me up over his shoulder in my next breath and slaps my ass again. "We're doing this right tonight."

"Oh my God." Cross takes the stairs two steps at a time as I hold in my excited giggle. "Pretty sure we've been doing it right all along. I've got no complaints."

"Such a brat." He walks into his room and drops me to his bed with a bounce, then turns back and locks his bedroom door. "I'm going to spread you out and eat you out before I make you scream for me, Everly. Then I'm going to fuck you until I'm the only god you pray to."

Oh fuck.

He unbuttons his starched dress shirt slowly as I watch, my mouth going dry with each new inch of exposed skin.

"Cat got your tongue, baby?"

"Forgive me, father, for I have sinned, and I'm about to do it again. Hopefully over and over and over." I press my hand under my panties and lie there with one leg straight, my toes pointed like a good little dancer, and one knee bent. My back arches, and my fingers slide through my wet sex . . . Waiting.

Cross looks like he about swallows his tongue as his lips curl up into a wicked grin. "You been playing with yourself a lot lately, Evie?"

"Maybe."

He grabs my ankles so fast my back slams against the bed while he drags me to the edge and drops to his knees. "Fuck that. I own your pussy, remember?"

Cross slides my panties down my legs, then shoves them in his pocket with that damn grin that makes me laugh before he throws my legs over his shoulders. His hands glide up my stomach, tracing my skin on their way to my breasts, which are exposed under his cropped t-shirt, before the tips of his tongue traces the seam of my sex.

Tasting. Teasing.

He adds one finger, then two.

Stroking my sex.

Gathering the wetness from between my legs, from my arousal that's been building for what seems like hours, thanks to the edging that started the second he saw me backstage at the fashion show. "Always so wet for me."

I whimper, and Cross slides two fingers inside me slowly. Almost lazily. And I arch up into him, already desperate for more.

I lean up on my elbows, needing to watch him.

To see the sinful sight of Cross Wilder's dark eyes piercing my soul from between my legs.

A scream lodges in my throat.

"The kids are asleep, and the doors are closed, Everly. But you've got to be quiet."

With shaky hands, I claw at the bed. Needing to grab something. Anything. To ground myself. I bite down hard on my bottom lip until I taste the first trickle of blood as my orgasm rips from the depths of my chest.

Cross grabs my waist and pulls me closer until I can't take it anymore.

"Cross . . . Please. Please. I need . . ." I can't breathe or think. "I need you."

"I know what you need, baby."

He kisses the inside of my thigh, then each of my hips as he makes his way up my body, stopping to drag his tongue along the underside of my exposed breasts. "I'm going to fuck you with my name on your body, Everly."

I shove his shirt off his shoulders and run my fingers over his chest. "What's this?"

Tucked among the cluster of tattoos on his ribcage is a new one. The tips of my fingers gently trace the design. "Cross..." I have no words.

"I had no idea when I met you how fitting Cinderella would be for you. For us. I'm no prince, Everly. But I will always search for you. Shoe or not. You can run if you have to. But I'll always find you."

My finger hovers on the tiny blue Cinderella slipper tucked tightly against a clockface striking midnight. "You put me on your body."

"You already own my soul, baby."

"I love you," I tell him as I pull at his belt, desperate for everything with this man.

Cross covers my mouth with his, worshipping me, and my belly tightens. Heat pools between my legs already. So fucking close again.

A wanton moan slips past my lips, and Cross steps back and finally takes off his pants and boxers before crawling between my bent thighs, whispering filthy words that set every inch of my body on fire.

He shoves my shirt up and sucks a deliciously sensitive nipple into his mouth, and *oh my God.*

"I need you," I murmur running my nails down the tight muscles of his back, and it might be the most emotionally raw thing I've ever said to him.

"I love you," he whispers before his next kiss steals my breath and owns my soul.

CROSS

I've never had this woman spread out before me on my bed, and wild horses couldn't get me to rush this. My hands mold to her body, worshipping every soft curve. Each dip and flare. I drag my tongue along her warm skin and revel in the way she shudders beneath me. Always so responsive. I run my teeth over her tight nipple, and she gasps and arches up. Her knees lock around me, and I run my hands down her thighs.

"Cross," she whimpers, trembling, and I flip us onto our sides, spooning. I cup her tight ass in my hands and throw her leg over my hip, opening her to me.

"Shh, baby. I've got you."

Everly's moan is beautiful when I tuck her against me, my arm curling around her shoulders, locking her in place. My lips devour hers as I slide home.

"Oh, God," she moans. I drag my tongue down her neck, sucking that sweet spot where it meets her shoulder, and she reaches back with her arm, grabbing my head.

One hand slides up to her throat and squeezes just enough, while the other plays with her clit. My girl hangs on tight as I fuck her fiercely. Mercilessly. Drowning in her. In us.

"Don't stop," she begs, like it was even an option.

"I promised you all night," I growl against her ear and fuck into her harder. Faster. Until she's shaking and keening and tightening around me.

"I want forever, Cross."

"Forever, baby." My own orgasm threatens, but it's not my turn yet. "You and me. I'm never letting go."

And that's what she needed to hear as her entire body tightens, clamping down on me before she comes with my name on her lips.

I fuck her through her orgasm as her pussy milks my cock, and my muscles coil and tighten. "So fucking pretty," I growl into her ear and turn her face to me, demanding her lips.

My tongue fucks her mouth in time with each snap of my hips until she stops shaking, then I pull out , flip her over, and smack her ass. "Ass in the air, baby."

Everly smiles and scrambles to her knees, putting that incredible fucking ass right in my face. Her t-shirt falls to just below her shoulder blades, and my name and number dominate her otherwise naked fucking body. "Goddamn. So hot," I growl and grip her hips.

"Cross . . ." She looks over her shoulder, her hair spilling to one side, and there's that grin again. "Don't be gentle."

Fuck, I love this woman.

I press the head of my cock against her swollen, wet cunt and ease in slowly, *so fucking slowly.*

A guttural whine rips from her throat as I hit a completely different spot from the new angle, and her breath catches in her throat. She drops her forehead to the mattress and pushes back against each thrust.

"So good, Cross."

Fire burns in my veins as I wrap an arm around her waist and control our movements. Moving her faster. Fucking her harder. With bruising thrusts, my muscles contract with each snap of my hips. Each sweet crash of our bodies coming together.

"Please, God. Cross," she begs and pleads with her fists full of the sheets under her. "I need . . ."

I smack her ass, then run my palm over the stinging red handprint. "I know what you need, baby."

With one hand, I stroke her clit until she's shaking again. Her come dripping between us. Soaking me. And I work that up to her perfect fucking ass. Her wild eyes fly to mine as my finger presses against her puckered skin and pushes inside her ass. She comes immediately, falling against the bed, and I don't wait for her to stop shaking before I pull my finger out and replace it with my cock.

She gasps, and those wild eyes I love fly wide to mine.

"Breathe, Everly. Tell me now if this isn't okay."

"Don't you dare stop now, Cross."

"Breathe out, baby."

Fuck. She's so tight as she pushes back against me, whimpering.

I run my thumb over her clit and stuff her pussy full with three fingers as I bottom out inside her ass. And holy shit. I've never felt anything tighter in my life.

Everly chants my name over and over as I lose myself in her. "Tell me you're mine, Everly. I want all of you. Your body. Your heart. Your fucking soul, Everly, I want it all."

"Oh, God," she pants. "Yours, Cross. Only ever yours. Now. Forever."

I wrap her hair around my fist and yank her up until her back is against my chest.

Everly reaches back and loops an arm around my neck, clinging to me.

We move together until we're moving as one.

Cum drips between us. We're sticky and sweaty and fucking desperate for each other.

And somehow, I still manage to hold off until she comes one more time for me before I pull out quickly.

Everly falls to the bed, and I grip my cock. A guttural sound rips from my chest, and her name falls from my lips, like a prayer. Hot thick ropes of cum jerk all over her naked ass, and bare back. Until it paints my name on her shirt.

I collapse next to her, and she crawls into my arms. Both of us so completely destroyed, there's no going back. There's no more running. No more chasing. It's just us. Together.

"Cross . . ." she whispers into the darkened, quiet room, her voice raw. Tears pool in her eyes.

"We've got our whole lives, Everly. Sleep now. I've got you."

"No more running," she whispers and closes her eyes.

Sometime before the sun rises, Everly lies on my chest, her naked body draped over mine, awake but soft and languid and barely moving. Hours of mind-blowing sex will do that to a person. If it weren't for her fingertips drawing lazy circles on my chest, I wouldn't even know she was awake until she flashes me those eyes I love.

"I don't know why you're so patient with me, Cross." The dejected tone in her voice breaks my fucking heart and makes me want to slay every one of her demons and bring their heads back to her as a prize.

"One day, you're going to tell me who hurt you, baby. You're going to let me shoulder that fucking burden for you. Because nothing should have as much control over you as

THE WILDCAT

you give this." I temper my words, so they sound gentle, even though inside, I feel anything but.

She lays her head on my chest and looks away. "I never had a serious boyfriend until college. And even then, I'm not sure if we were ever actually serious, or if it was just convenient. He knew my friends, and that's where I drew my line. I didn't bring him around my family. I never did. When you grow up in a family like mine, people like to use you. Either so they can say they know this group of athletes, or they want to use you to get to them, in the hope to use them for something. It always drove Keith nuts that I wouldn't bring him to games or family dinners, so we ended up being one of those dramatic couples who broke up every other month. But we were together, on and off, almost all four years. More off than on, if I'm honest."

A chill skates down my back. I already don't like where this is going, but I keep my mouth shut and tangle a hand in her hair, rubbing the base of her skull. I need to tread carefully and guard my reactions or I have no doubt she'll freeze up.

"By graduation weekend, we'd been off for a little while, and I promised the girls I wasn't getting back together with him . . ." She sits up and tucks the sheet around herself. "They weren't big fans of his. But we had friends in common."

"So that was what? Two years ago?"

"Not quite." She sighs deeply, and her shoulders shake. "It will be two years next June. I hadn't seen him for a while by then. He'd called a few times, but I was just done. You know what I mean? When you get to that point with someone where you don't want to do the on-off thing anymore. It's just over. We ran into him and a few friends at the bar. We all partied together, but every time he'd try to dance with me, I'd move away. I didn't flirt. We didn't hook up, and I know I told him I wasn't interested more than once, but he never was good at being told no."

Goddammit. No. Please God, don't let this woman be about to tell me this.

"We'd all been friends since freshmen year in college, so we didn't think anything of it and went back to the house when the bar closed. Back then, the five of us lived in a house off campus. But it was just Brynn and me that night."

My blood is boiling with a rage that's going to be someone's destruction.

I'm going to find this guy, rip his dick off, and use it to beat him to death with my bare fucking hands.

"The last thing I remember is the room swimming around me and then thinking I needed to go to bed." She chews her bottom lip as tears pool in her aquamarine eyes. "I woke up the next morning naked. Keith was lying next to me in bed. He was naked too. And I couldn't remember anything. It wasn't like a hangover. It was a blackout." She straightens her shoulders and swallows. "I've been drunk before, Cross. But I've never blacked out. And I hadn't had that much to drink. It wasn't adding up, but it felt like my brain was muddled."

"Fuck, Everly." I move so I can wrap my arm around her, but she inches away.

"Just let me get through this, okay?"

"Whatever you need, baby."

Her smile is small and so fucking broken, violence burns in my veins.

"He tried to convince me we hooked up. No big deal, same as always. But the thing is . . . I knew in my heart he was lying."

"Everly . . ." I cup her beautiful face in my hands and gently wipe away the tears streaming down her cheeks. "You don't have to keep going if this is too hard."

As if I hadn't spoken a word, she stares right past me. "I

stayed in bed all morning. Until he left. Until the house quieted and I was sure I was the only one home. Then I sat in the shower and cried for hours. Until the water ran cold, and my skin was wrinkled and freezing. I couldn't move. I couldn't even try. Because hours after I woke up naked and sore, my memory started to come back to me in pieces. Not the whole night. Never everything. I still don't remember that much. But it came back in . . . in flashes. Like slides of an old grainy home video." She turns in my arms and stares right into my eyes.

"I told him no, Cross. I know I did. But we'd been together for years, and he thought I was just playing hard to get. That's what he kept saying. *Don't play hard to get now, Everly.*"

My voice gets lost in my fucking throat.

"He drugged me, and he had sex with me while I was too out of it to stop him. And it was my fault."

"It was not your fault, Everly. He drugged you, and he raped you. You said no while you could, and he waited until you couldn't to take advantage of you. None of that is your fault."

"I trusted him, Cross. I let him into my life, and I trusted him. If I hadn't—"

"No means no, Everly. And if you weren't able to say no, then it shouldn't have even been an option. No. It's an entire sentence. It's all you ever should have had to say, and if you couldn't fucking say it, then it should have been automatic, baby." I'm trying so fucking hard to watch the anger in my voice, so I don't scare my girl and she doesn't shut down. "He attacked you, Everly. Did you ever tell anyone? The girls? The police? Your family?"

"Brynlee knows. But that's it. My father . . . my brothers . . . the guys . . . any one of them would have killed him. Actually physically killed him, and I couldn't live with the consequences of their actions on their lives and on my conscience. *They would have killed him, Cross.*"

"So he's still out there, free?"

"Yes." She freezes, her eyes locked on mine. "And that's how he's going to stay. Because I'm not digging this up now."

The Philly Press

KROYDON KRONICLES

ANOTHER ONE BITES THE DUST

All the beautiful who's who of Kroydon Hills were at the Le Désir fashion show last night. So many Kroydon Kouples, past and present, dressed up in their evening best to watch a new wave of *It* girls strut their stuff on the super-sexy black and silver runway. But it was the finale that left this reporter speechless. Everyone's favorite new, notoriously private *It* couple made a statement in a big way when Everly Sinclair strutted her stuff adorned with Cross Wilder's name and number. Looks like another one bit the dust. Are you team #WildSin for life? I'm here for it.
#KroydonKronicles

CROSS

"We'll see you in a few hours, baby." I pull Everly close to me and press my lips to hers. "Love you."

Everly smiles, but it doesn't reach her eyes as she runs her fingers through my hair. "Love you too." She moves next to me and squats down in front of Kerrigan. "Listen, little miss. Gracie is going to stop by with a present for you, okay?"

"A present?" Her eyes grow wide. "For me?"

"Yes, ma'am." Everly kisses the top of Kerrigan's head. "I'll see you guys after the game. I'll meet you in the suite."

Kerrigan and I watch her leave, and I look at my daughter and say a silent prayer that I can keep her safe forever.

Hours later, Ares, Bellamy, and I walk into the Sinclair's private suite at Kings Stadium with both kids and enough toys, bottles, and baby accessories for it to look more like we're moving in than coming for a few hours.

Annabelle is the first to see us, and she makes a beeline straight for Kerrigan. "Hey, sweet girl. I see you got your present."

Kerrigan spins around in a little circle, smiling as her pink, sparkly tutu spins out around her. Gracie stopped by earlier with the tutu, and a black Kings jersey with Sinclair and the number eighty-one in pink sparkles on the back. Apparently, that's Callen's number.

And then, because according to Grace, every girl needs them, she also gave Kerrigan a sparkly pink pair of Doc Martens. My three-year-old is now dressed more fashionably than I am.

"You look so pretty. Are you hungry?" Annabelle asks and holds out her hand.

Kerrigan looks to me for permission. "You can go with Mrs. Sinclair, sweetie."

She quietly takes Annabelle's hand and squeals when she tells her there're cupcakes just for her, and I watch as Kerrigan's led toward a group of women, including the owner of Sweet Temptations, who's standing next to Grace.

Seeing Grace makes me breathe a little easier.

Caitlin grabs Bellamy, and they move to the outside seats as Ares and I hang back. "You want a beer, Cross?"

"No. Not until I get the all clear to skate," I tell my brother and then unbuckle Jax from his carrier and pick him up.

The suite is full of Everly's family, including her father, who comes over once I've got Jax settled. "Cross."

"Mr. Sinclair," I answer awkwardly.

"Seriously, call me Declan."

"Okay."

He looks at me for a long moment. "Annabelle said I had to be nice."

"Remind me to thank your wife." Jax whines in my arms until I fish his binky out of the car seat and pop it in his mouth.

"You don't talk much, do you?" he asks as he orders a bourbon from the bartender in the corner of the suite.

"Not really." Guess it's time to man up though. "But I meant what I said last night. I love your daughter, sir."

"Don't call me *sir*. I'm already in denial that my baby is old enough to be dating a man with babies of his own. Sir makes it worse." He looks over to where Annabelle has Kerrigan standing on a chair so she can see better. "You'll see. They grow up so damn fast. One day, they're wearing the tutu and your jersey and the next day they're dancing for your team in the tiniest uniform you've ever seen, and their boyfriend is bringing his family to the game in the tutu and jersey."

That raises my hackles. "We can leave—"

"Don't. That didn't come out how it was meant to. Gracie says you're a really good guy. So does Belle. And my boys like you too. I'm just having a hard time accepting Everly in an adult relationship. Are you coming to dinner at my house after this?"

"Yes, sir. I mean, yes. We are. It was nice of you to invite us today. We won't get many weekends where we can come to a game once the season starts." Jax spits out his binky, and Declan laughs and picks it up, then tosses it into the car seat. "Here." He puts his hands out. "Why don't you let me hold him. Everly is about to come on the field. You don't want to miss my girl doing her thing."

The look he gives me is sad. "Doesn't matter how old they get, Cross. They're always your girl. Enjoy them when they're little and still think you hung the damn moon."

I carefully give him Jax and watch Declan's eyes light up

when Jax yanks his hair. "What do you say, Jaxon? Maybe you'll like football better than hockey, unlike my kids."

Doubtful. But I keep that to myself as I walk up to the glass and watch a giant kickline of cheerleaders marching out onto the field in only slightly more clothing than Everly wore on stage last night. And damn, she's incredible. The way she moves. The way she smiles. She lights up out there, brighter than the brightest star.

"Daddy," Kerrigan squeals again. "Look at Miss Evie. Look how pretty she looks, Daddy."

"She's perfect," I whisper, and Declan claps my shoulder.

"Nobody's perfect, Cross. But she's pretty damn close. So don't fuck it up."

I don't bother correcting him.

But he's wrong.

Everly is perfect.

Perfect for me. For us.

And I'm not fucking this up because that woman is the love of my life.

---

*B*efore the end of the first quarter, the suite is full of people. Everly's family is big. And full of football players. Two of her uncles played for Maryland before they retired. Her godfather played for the Kings. And another uncle is apparently a former Navy SEAL, who warned me that he didn't need Sam Beneventi to kill me if I hurt Everly. He knew 131 ways to kill a man and dispose of a body without ever being caught.

Finally, I gave in and asked Sam, who's Maddox's dad, why everyone uses him as a threat.

Maddox laughs at me right before his father smacks the

back of his head. "Comes with the job," he tells me and walks away.

"What's his job?" I ask Maddox.

"Waste management," he says with a straight face, then follows his dad.

Wait . . . like . . . ?

Kerrigan runs over and throws her arms up in the air until I pick her up. "Daddy . . . is it almost over?"

"Soon, baby," I tell her and kiss the top of her head.

"Hey there, little lady," Everly's brother Leo says as he moves next to us. "Are you having fun at your first game?"

She nods her head, the space buns Bellamy put in her hair bobbling with the movement.

"How about you, man? Are you a football guy?" Leo reminds me of Ares. He's tall and lean but muscular. Everly mentioned he's a hockey player at Kroydon University, and I can see it.

"I mean, it's not hockey, but it's not bad," I tell him.

He takes a pull of his beer and watches Callen make a great catch. "Yeah, I'm with you. Pretty sure Dad cried when he ended up with three hockey players instead of football stars."

"Yeah. I could see that."

"I still feel kinda shitty about what I said at the girls' place a few weeks ago. It really did just come out wrong. It's pretty cool seeing Everly bring you around the family. Especially the whole family. I've only ever met one guy she's dated, and that's because I played hockey with him, not because she brought him around the family."

Warning bells go off in my mind. I probably shouldn't ask, but I fucking have to.

"Yeah? Did you play with him in high school or college?" Inside, I'm praying Leo says high school. He's only two years younger than Everly. It could have been high school.

"College. Keith was on KU's team before Pittsburgh drafted him." Leo cheers as the Kings score, and my head feels like it's being split in two. But this isn't from the fucking concussion.

"Keith . . ." Keith who got drafted by Pittsburgh two years ago. "Keith fucking Dolan?"

You've got to be kidding me.

"Yeah, man. But seriously. Don't sweat it. He's good, but he's no you. And like I said, she never even introduced him to Mom and Dad. That's got to be one of those girl tests, right?" Leo keeps talking, but the goddamn wind tunnel in my head drowns him out.

Now I know why hockey is a problem for her.

Keith fucking Dolan was a first-round draft pick the year they graduated.

And I'm going to fucking kill him.

Everly

When Cross told me he was invited to dinner, I should have known my mother would invite the entire family. And by entire, I mean everyone. Aunts, uncles, cousins. They're all here, and they're all loud, and Kerrigan hasn't moved from my hip since we walked in the door and she looked at me with her big overwhelmed eyes.

"I'm sorry," I whisper in Cross's ear. He's been strangely quiet, even for him, since we got here. "We can leave as soon as you're ready."

"It's fine" is all the answer I get before he walks away, leaving me to wonder what the hell happened between this morning and now.

"Hey." Grace hip-checks me. "What's going on with you and . . ." She looks at Kerrigan, then over to Cross, who's talking with Callen and Maddox.

I shrug. "No clue. Was everything okay at the game?"

"As far as I saw." Gracie grabs Leo and Hendrix as they walk by. "Did anything happen with . . ." Gracie nods toward Cross, not wanting to say his name in front of Kerrigan.

"Is she having a seizure?" Hendrix asks Leo.

"Is that a new dance move or something, Gracie?" Leo asks, and I'm pretty sure the dumbass is serious.

I shake my head. "You two are awful."

"Whatever." Hendrix holds his hands up for Kerrigan. "Hey, Kerri girl. Want to go play on the swings with me?"

Kerrigan looks at me, like she wants my approval, and I smile back at her when I see a few of my little cousins outside.

"Do not let a single hair on her head get hurt or I will castrate you," I whisper to my brother and move Kerrigan from my hip to his.

"Always so violent, evil twin."

I scratch my nose with my middle finger as he walks away and wonder why anyone trusts any of us with their kids when we act like overgrown babies ourselves sometimes.

As soon as he's gone, Grace shoves Leo up against the bookcase. "Spill it, superstar."

"Aww . . . I am a superstar, aren't I?" He smiles big, and I think I'm gonna kill him.

"Shut up, Leo. It just sounded good. Now tell us if something happened during the game today. You were with Cross the most." Grace tries her hand at interrogation, but it doesn't really work. It's more like a ladybug yelling at a cockroach. Not exactly effective. But kinda funny to watch.

"Nothing that I saw. We talked about football and hockey.

And how Everly never brought Keith around the family." Leo smiles, and my stomach bottoms out. "Oh, and he wanted to know what the hell Uncle Sam actually does. You know, I still don't know how to answer that. I mean, it's not like we can say he's the godfather."

"Leo. Shut up," I whisper with a hand on his chest. "You said Keith. Back up to there."

"Yeah, Keith. Why?"

Every hair on my body stands on edge. "Why were you talking about Keith?"

"I just told him you never brought him around. That Cross is the only guy you've ever trusted with the family. Pretty much the same shit I told him before. I mean, seriously, what am I supposed to say to the guy? *Hey, congrats on bagging my sister. Good job.* Doesn't really work that way." He moves to walk away, but I step in his way.

"Leo," I push him back, and he lets me. "Did you say Keith's name? Like his actual name?"

"Jesus, Evie. Chill the fuck out. Your man has been in the NHL for a decade. He's not gonna get all freaked-out because your ex went first round in the draft."

"Did you use his name?" I seethe through gritted teeth.

"He did," a voice answers from behind me, and I cringe.

This is so bad.

EVERLY

The car ride back to Cross's house is driven in silence. Luckily, Bellamy was crashing on campus tonight with Caitlin, and Ares took his own car to the stadium, so he could skip dinner after and do whatever he does when he's not home. He and I have a don't ask, don't tell understanding. It's working so far. That left Cross and me and the kids, who both zonked out during the short drive from my parents' back to their house.

The stormy sky looks ominous, which is pretty fucking fitting because the tension in the car is thick enough to cut with a dull butter knife. The awkward silence continues once the car is parked. Cross grabs Kerrigan, and I take Jax. We bring them both into the house, get them changed, and put them to bed.

Kerrigan goes without a problem, but Jax wants a bottle and a snuggle before he'll let me put him down, and even then, I don't want to let him go. Because once I do, I'm going to have to deal with his daddy. And I'm not sure how I feel about that. Fear is warring with anger, and I have no clue which is going to win out.

Cross watches me from Jax's open doorframe, not saying a word as I rock his son, soaking in his sweet baby scent. Trying to enjoy the calm innocence before the storm brewing inside and out explodes around us.

Once I'm sure he's asleep, I lay him down in his crib and follow Cross into his bedroom. He's sitting on his bed with his head in his hands when I walk in, and my stomach bottoms out as I reach for him. "Cross..."

"Don't, Everly," he bites back softly, but there's no mistaking the anger in his tone. An anger I'm not used to hearing from him. "Were you ever going to tell me?"

"Tell you what?" I wrap my arms around myself defensively.

"Keith Dolan?" He looks up at me, and his onyx eyes are raging with the heat of a thousand scorched suns. His anger is so visceral, I have to look away before I get burned. "I know him. I play against him at the end of the week. How could you not tell me it was him?"

"What?" I step back, feeling the stinging slap of his words against my skin. "How could I not tell you? You're kidding me, right?"

He looks completely wrecked when his eyes meet mine. "I promise you, baby, there isn't a single thing about this I find funny. I want to kill him. Like with my bare fucking hands, kill him."

"This isn't about you, Cross. It never was. I didn't tell you who he was because I didn't want you or anyone else to know. And what you just said is my number one reason for keeping it to myself. If you kill him. Or hurt him. Or do anything stupid... If you do any of that, it ruins your life. It could potentially ruin the kids' lives. And I have to go through the hell of reopening myself up to all this again. It's not worth it. *He's* not worth it. You are. And I refuse to let you get in trouble because of me."

Cross runs his hands through his hair, tugging on it, frustration obviously eating him alive. "I will always protect you. You and the kids. You're my world. Making sure you're safe will always . . . *always* be my number one priority. And this piece of shit made you feel unsafe. He took advantage of you. He—"

"Don't." I hold out a shaky hand, stopping him. "Don't say it. I know what *he* did, Cross. I've lived with it. I've dealt with it. I've moved on. You don't get to be mad at me because now you know who he is." I ignore everything else he's said. It's so much easier to be mad at him right now, instead of feeling hurt or scared or guilt-stricken, even though I'm feeling all those things, rolled into one big, ugly black ball of pain and grief.

"But have you, Everly? Have you dealt with it?" Cross stands and moves in front of me, but he's smart enough not to touch me.

Not yet.

Not right now.

"Yes. I've dealt with it. I talked to a therapist for a year, Cross. I've dealt with it. It might not be the way you want me to have. But I did deal with it. And I seriously can't believe we're arguing about this." I'm so angry, I could scream or cry or hit something.

Any of those options work right now.

"Then why is he still walking around a free fucking man, baby? Why didn't you go to the police? How could you not press charges?" he yells at me.

Actually yells, and I shrink in on myself for a second before anger blooms and I fight back. "No. You do not get to decide how I handle this. You weren't there," I snap, my stomach churning and threatening to bring up everything I've eaten today. "This didn't happen to you. It happened to *me*. And I don't want the world to know about it. I don't want to tell my family. I don't want my father and my brothers to look at me differently. I don't want people to pity me. Or some troll on social media to wonder whether I'm lying or trying to get attention. I choose what I want to do. And I dealt with it how I wanted to."

Cross moves into my space and gently cups my face in his hands. "Baby . . . what would you do if someone hurt Kerrigan the way he hurt you? Wouldn't you want him arrested? Prosecuted? Convicted? Wouldn't you want to make sure he couldn't do the same thing to anyone else ever again? Every day this motherfucker is free is another day he can hurt someone else."

"Low blow, Cross. Yes. I would want anyone who hurt her to be punished. I'd want him to be thrown in prison and the key thrown away. But I'm not your daughter," I yell back at him.

Cross's eyes flare before he roars back at me, "No. You're the love of my life. And I can't fix this for you. Let me fix this."

"It's not your job to fix me, Cross." I grab my purse and pull out my keys.

"What are you doing?" Cross moves around me, blocking the bedroom door, and I step around him. "Don't do this, Everly. Don't run."

"I'm not going to stand here and take this. I'm not going to let you yell at me over something I have no control over."

"You have all the control, Everly. All of it. You can make sure he never does this again."

I grab the doorknob and wait for him to move, only he doesn't.

"You promised me twenty-four hours ago that you wouldn't run. No more running . . . remember?"

"Move, Cross," I warn and yank the door open.

"Everly . . . don't do this." His voice shreds the last solid strands of my soul.

"I can't do this, Cross." I walk around him, then hurry down the steps and through the front door, slamming it behind me. I race off the porch and stop for a split-second, wondering what I'm doing before the heavens open and blanket me in a cold sheet of rain.

I stare into the dark, starless sky with a scream building in my throat. It mixes with a sob, and my knees threaten to buckle while tears mix with rain and pour down my face. *Fuck.*

Being mad is so much easier.

Running is easier.

But I love him.

Cross is worth harder.

He's worth the work.

He's worth the struggle.

He's worth everything, and I just ran again.

I stand there, locked in place and freezing, knowing I just made the biggest mistake of my life.

Cross

By the time the front door slams shut behind her, I know I need to stop her. No way she's leaving without a fight. I speed down the steps and throw open the door in time to hear a guttural, pain-filled scream ripped violently from her throat.

I want so badly to go to her, but I wait.

She needs this.

So I move slowly instead of rushing.

Softly, instead of pushing.

Basically, the opposite of what I've just done.

I whisper her name, "Everly . . . baby."

She turns to see me, her gorgeous cheeks red and streaked with tears as the storm pounds down against us both. Everly bites her lip, and a weary, sad smile graces her gorgeous face. "You chased me . . ." she cries.

"I'll always chase you, baby. I'll always find you. And I'll always bring you home. To me and the kids. You're my forever, Everly Sinclair."

"And you're my home, Cross Wilder." She runs her hands through her rain-soaked hair and laughs. "We've got a thing for the rain, don't we?"

I wrap my arms around her and kiss her head. "It washes everything away so we can start fresh."

"I don't think I can go to the police, Cross. I don't want everyone to know what happened to me." Hiccups rack her tiny body as another sob breaks from her lips.

My heart constricts at the sound of my girl breaking in front of me. "You don't have to do anything you don't want, Everly. Never again. I promise. I won't push."

She grips me like a lifeline holding her head above water. Like I'm the only thing keeping her together, and I swear to whatever fucked up thing in this universe that allowed this to happen to her that I'll make it right.

I scoop her up in my arms and carry her inside, then walk us upstairs and turn the hot water on in the shower before putting us both inside, fully clothed.

"Cross," she sputters.

"You're freezing cold, baby. Let me take care of you. Please . . ."

Her eyes soften, and she nods silently.

I carefully strip her out of her clothes, then do the same to myself.

There's nothing sexual about it. This is me taking care of her.

Everly goes through the motions, lifting her arms and turning to let me wash her hair.

She doesn't speak. Doesn't cry.

After, I wrap her in a towel and lay her down in our bed. She curls around me and closes her eyes instantly. My gorgeous girl is safe and asleep and wrapped in my arms, where I'll never let anything hurt her again. Not even me.

That's when I start to plan.

And it's not until I hear Ares, hours later, that I put it in motion.

Everly's Secret Thoughts

Never say you can't do something.
Say you haven't done it yet.
That yet is important.

EVERLY

Two days later, I meet Lindy and a realtor in front of an old two-story white Victorian-inspired storefront on the corner of Main Street. It's a few storefronts down from Le Désir and one block down from my Mom's studio. I asked Lindy to meet me here because her family owns the building. It's been empty for a few months, and Lindy mentioned before that it was under contract for a high-end architect, but the contract fell through.

She's got Griffin in some kind of crazy-looking wrap thing strapped to her chest, and the little man is kicking his feet, thrilled with life. It makes my heart pang for Jaxon, who I left with Mrs. Ashburn this morning while Cross is at physical therapy with Brynn. His head seems fine. But his vision is still giving him problems.

Once the realtor gets the door open, we walk inside, and I'm struck immediately by the natural lighting and beautiful shapes of the building. The rounded pointed turret on the end of the building would make the perfect place to highlight whatever design I wanted spotlighted. The windows are huge boxes. And the bones of the building are stunning. Wide plank hardwood floors and soaring ten-foot ceilings.

"This is one of the few remaining original mansions from when Kroydon Hills was incorporated, nearly 150 years ago," the realtor tells us, and I link my fingers with Lindy's and drag her around behind me.

We walk through the whole first floor in awe, then go upstairs, and I stop and stare. "Lindy . . . please tell me your family will sell me this building."

My best friend smiles. "Listen, I'll make you a deal. I'll get King Corp. to sell you the building if you'll let me work for you. I can't stand not working, and I haven't figured out what I want to do. But Evie . . . this. This, I could do. Let me handle the business side of things while you handle the designs. We don't need to be partners. I'll work for you. But give me a chance to show you how I can help."

"Are you serious?" I ask in shock that she'd even consider working with me.

She's an heiress. A literal billionaire.

"I have so much to learn, Linds," I tell her, then practically hold my breath. "I'd rather have a partner than an employee."

"Really?" she screeches. "I don't bring a ton of experience to the table, but my contribution can be the building."

"Lindy, I can't let you do that."

"Yes, you can. It's my investment." She drags me to one of the upstairs bedrooms. "Look. This can be your office, with the big windows overlooking the park. And the one back there can be mine. Maybe we could even turn one of these rooms into a kids' room, so I could get a nanny and have her come here a few days a week."

My smile grows, thinking about it. "That's a great idea. Wow. We're really going to do this?"

She nods excitedly. "Who knows? Maybe you could bring Jax or Kerrigan sometimes too."

"Maybe," I softly agree.

"Rumor has it you haven't been sleeping at the condo."

I blow out a breath. "Rumor, huh?"

"Pesky things." She smirks, and I shake my head.

"It's not official. I haven't moved out or anything. Not yet," I add, not sure what the hell Cross and I are doing . . . not yet.

"That *yet* is important," she tells me.

"Yeah, that *yet* is important."

I pick Cross up from physical therapy that afternoon, and he's grinning like a loon. "How was PT, big man?"

He gets in the car, his smile stretching from ear to ear. "I got the all clear. I'm going to be back on the ice for the season opener tomorrow night."

My heart soars, then sinks.

Game one.

He's going to play in the game against Pittsburgh.

The game against Keith.

He's dropped it since our fight Sunday night, but we both know what this means.

"That's fantastic, Wilder," I tell him with my best cheerleady excitement. "Please be careful though. I like your brain the way it is."

"You think you might want to come?" he asks, but even without the lack of enthusiasm, I'm sure he knows there's no way I'm going. Not to *that game* in particular.

"I'd rather not. Maybe another game," I offer as we head back to the house. "But I'll watch it on TV."

THE WILDCAT

"Yeah?" He sounds hopeful, and I feel like an asshole. But it's the best I can do.

"Yeah. I'll see if any of the girls are around. I know Lindy's going to the game, but the others might not be. Or maybe I'll watch it with my mom. She's always looking for an excuse to spend time together."

"You're going to be okay, baby," he tells me soothingly.

"I know. Want to hear about the new shop?" I ask, changing the subject to a topic that doesn't make me want to puke.

"Do you have a name for it yet?"

I shake my head. "Not yet."

"You could make it Everly Amelia. Do the whole two-name thing. Like Ralph Lauren or Donna Karen."

"I'm impressed you even know who either of those designers are." I mean, my man wears clothes well. But he doesn't know anything at all about fashion.

"I pay attention." When I cock my head his way, he laughs. "I pay attention to you. Not to fashion."

"I love you, baby," I giggle as we turn into the driveway.

"Hey. What's Gracie doing here?" I hop out of the car and look at hers sitting in the driveway.

Cross shrugs. "Let's go find out."

When we get inside, she's sitting on the couch in a tiara with Kerrigan and Ares. Yes, Ares is wearing a tiara too. Oh, man. I need to get a picture of this.

"Hey, guys. What are you watching?"

"*Cinderella*," Kerrigan tells us with her sweet, quiet voice.

Bellamy comes rushing into the room, fixing her crown, with a sleeping Jax on her shoulder. "Don't start without me."

"Come watch wif us, Evie?" Kerrigan asks, and my heart warms.

"Sure, baby." I move around the couch and sit next to

Kerrigan. Then Cross rounds the couch with another tiara. He smiles and places it on my head.

"Cinderella needs her tiara, doesn't she, baby girl?"

Kerrigan giggles. "She does, Daddy."

Then he drops to one knee in front of me, and I stop breathing completely.

"She needs something else too." He pulls a Tiffany blue box from his pocket, and his eyes water when he cracks it open. "Baby..."

"Yes, Daddy?"

Cross laughs at his daughter but keeps his eyes on me. "My life is complicated. And loving me means loving more than just me. But it means you'll be loved by me."

"And me," Kerrigan pipes in. "And Jax too," she adds, so excited that I feel my first tear fall. Good tears this time.

"I love you, Everly Amelia Sinclair. Would you do me the honor of marrying me and loving us?"

"Oh, Cross." I drop to my knees in front of him and gather his face in my hands. "I already love all of you. Yes. I'll marry you."

He captures my lips with his, and Kerrigan giggles before Cross pulls back and slips a gorgeous, brilliant-cut diamond solitaire on my finger. "A perfect fit," he says as he runs his finger over the ring.

"It's perfect, Cross," I gasp and try unsuccessfully to hold back my tears.

"Well, Gracie may have helped with that," he tells me, and my sister smiles.

"Thanks for letting me be here for this," she tells him with matching tears in her own eyes.

"Everly Wilder," I tell him.

"You gonna take my name, baby?" he murmurs, so damn happy.

"Yup. And that's going to be the name. Everly Wilder Design."

My heart settles in a way I'm not sure it ever has before when Kerrigan, my quiet girl, jumps up on the couch, throws her arms wide open, and announces, "And they lived happily ever after."

I should have known it wouldn't be that easy.

CROSS

"Wilder," Kingston calls out after we finish our morning skate.

We already hit the ice for about thirty minutes this morning. Just enough to get a feel for the ice. Most of us are either going home to take a nap or going to see Brynn and Doc for treatment before we have to be back tonight for the game. Emotions are already riding high since our first home game of the season is against Pittsburgh. Two Pennsylvania teams. It's a grudge match every game between us. And that's before I wanted to kill their center.

"Wilder, slow down." I turn in the parking lot and see Jace coming toward me. We're two of the last guys to leave. Have been since he made me assistant captain.

"Sorry, Kingston. What's up? You need something?"

"Ares said something earlier."

We stop in front of my truck, and I turn his way. "Ignore him. Ares is usually goofing off anyway. But fuck if you'll find a better enforcer on the ice."

"Yeah." Jace crosses his arms over his chest and looks almost uncomfortable. "That's the thing. He mentioned something about you having a grudge to settle against Dolan."

"Motherfucker," I mumble under my breath. "Ignore him, Cap. It's all good."

"You're one of the top scorers on the team, Wilder. You can't get hurt on the back of a concussion. You could be out for the season." He waits for me to say something, and when I don't, he groans. "Fuck. He was serious, wasn't he? You have a problem on the ice, you let Ares handle it. It can't be you."

"He hurt someone I care about, Kingston. It's personal." My hands ball into tight fists, and the anger that's been growing for days swells. "It's not up to Ares to handle."

Jace looks me over. Calculating. "Heard you got engaged. Congratulations, man. I've known Everly Sinclair since she had skinned knees and braids and was on my kid sister's soccer team. She's a good girl. You're a lucky man."

"Thank you." I don't say anything else.

I don't need Jace to get in trouble if something goes wrong tonight.

"He hurt someone you care about?"

"Yeah, Cap." A muscle in my jaw ticks, and I bite back the rest of what I want to say.

"You going to destroy him the first chance you get?"

"Yeah. Could get me thrown out of the game. Might be looking at a suspension." I figure at this point, I might as well be honest. What do I have to lose?

"Let me see if I can get Coach to put you, me, and Ares on the first line tonight. I'll come up with a reason. They always start Dolan. Maybe we can get this done between the three of us without anyone getting suspended. Work for you?"

"Yeah. I'd appreciate that." I open the door of the truck before he leans against the side of it.

"How hard are you going after him?" he asks, having no fucking clue of the lengths I'd go to.

"If I could slice his neck with my skate and watch him bleed out in front of me on the fucking ice, I would. Since that's not an option, I'll have to settle for breaking him." I get in the truck and shut the door, done with this conversation.

I want to go home, get some sleep, and get back here to put some of Everly's demons to rest.

"*Hey*, big guy." Everly sits on the bed waking me later that afternoon. I lift my arm, and she crawls right into my side, resting her head on my chest. "How was your morning skate?"

"Good. Team skated well. Should be a good game. You going to your Mom's to watch it?" I press my lips to her head.

"Yeah. I think so. Grace might stop by if she gets out of rehearsal in time, but Kenzie and Lindy are going to the game. Obviously, Brynn is already going to be there."

"You don't have to watch it, baby." I'd actually prefer she not watch. But she's going to find out what happens either way.

"No. I want to watch you." She runs her hand under my shirt and presses against my heart. "I told Mrs. Ashburn I'd take the kids with me, if that's okay with you."

"Of course it's okay. I really appreciate the way your mom and dad were with the kids last weekend." And I mean it. They were amazing, and the kids seemed to take to them. Something Kerrigan seems to do easily with Everly's family.

"Oh, my parents are in love. My mom already asked if the kids can call her *Gigi*. She said Mrs. Sinclair is ridiculous. She wants to be a grandparent."

Well fuck. I may have just fallen in love with Everly's mom. "Really?"

"I know you asked my dad for permission to propose, Cross. Are you really telling me he didn't mention anything about the kids?"

"He said something about us all being family. But we're guys, Evie, we don't talk about feelings like that."

"I like it when you call me Evie." She smiles, and there isn't anything in the world I wouldn't do for that smile.

"Noted," I tell her and pull the blanket up around us. I still have another hour to sleep before I've got to get ready for the game.

"Lindy and I signed contracts today, and I gave my aunt my notice. I'll be done working for them in two weeks," she tells me softly.

"I'm so fucking proud of you, baby. Are you going to design your own wedding dress?"

"Of course. I always wanted to be a late June bride." She beams, and I feel like the Grinch. My heart grows ten times its size.

"Late June? That's specific."

"Can't get married until your season is over. And I think you're going all the way this year." She tips her head back and ghosts her lips over mine. "I can't wait to call you my husband."

"Love you, baby."

"Forever, Cross. No more running."

Let's hope she still feels that way after tonight.

Everly

I knock on the door of my parents' house, then walk in with the kids, calling out, "Hello..."

"Hello," Kerrigan mimics me in her tiny voice, and I hold back my laugh. She's certainly coming out of her shell, one baby step at a time, and I'm loving watching her do it. "Evie, are there cupcakes?"

"Did somebody say cupcakes?" Mom asks as she scoops Kerrigan up in a hug. "Why yes, little miss. There are cupcakes. I stopped by Miss Amelia's shop today and got a whole box for you to pick from. Do you want to see?"

Kerrigan nods her head excitedly and takes Mom's hand without looking for permission, and I think a tiny piece of my heart cracks.

I walk into the family room to drop all the kids' stuff and stop and stare.

I think Target may have thrown up at my parents' house.

"What's all this?" I ask Dad, who's already watching TV with Uncle Tommy.

"We're brushing up on hockey, Evie. I know college hockey for the boys. But I need to know pro hockey for Cross, if he's going to be family."

I push down the overwhelming emotion sitting on my chest and move around the couch to kiss my uncle. "This is why you're my favorite, Uncle Tommy."

"Do you know Cross has been the top scorer for the Revolution for the past two years? He beat Jace Kingston, who held the record for five years before Cross took it from him."

"No," I laugh. "I didn't know that."

"Well then, we can both learn hockey together," Tommy adds, and I smile when I realize he's wearing Cross's jersey. He's always been a die-hard Kings football fan. And when my uncles played for Kroydon U, he was the biggest college fan there ever was. But seeing him go all-in for the Revolution because Cross . . . because my future husband is on the team. Okay, yeah. It does squishy, melty things to my heart.

"How's my little buddy doing?" Dad asks as he unbuckles Jax from the car seat carrier.

Jax looks at Dad with big blue eyes and a tiny, trembling lip. "He's gonna cry, Dad."

"Nah, he loves me. We're buds," Dad swears just before Jax opens his mouth and screams. "Okay, buddy. Let's see what Belles got for you because she basically bought out the baby section of Target. There's got to be something here to make you happy."

"Did you put all this together?" I ask, and Tommy laughs.

"Nope. Your mom hired a task rabbit guy to do it, and your dad's pissed."

Okay, that makes me laugh and Dad grumble.

"I could have done it myself," he says under his breath.

Mom walks in with a tray of snacks and Kerrigan at her side with a plate of cookies. "Sure you could have, Dec. But this was faster." Then she lowers her voice and adds, "And with way less bitching."

She and Kerrigan put the plates on the coffee table, then Mom turns her to see the wall of pink that I'm pretty sure didn't come from Target. "Mom?" I question as Kerrigan makes her way over to a pink kitchen set.

"What?" Mom shrugs. "So I stopped by Pottery Barn Kids too. Let me spoil them." Then she goes right back over to Kerrigan and sits on the floor with her, where I have no doubt, she'll stay for the entire game.

"We have pretty great parents."

I gasp and turn and shove Leo as hard as I can. "You scared the shit out of me."

"Language, Everly. There's little ears," Mom scolds, and I, in turn, yank on Leo's ear.

"Ow. Hey, what's that for?"

"That's for scaring me. What are you doing here?" I demand while my eyes go back and forth between Kerrigan and Mom, and Dad and Jax.

"Your laundry is in the dryer, Leo. I haven't folded it yet. But if you bring it in here for me, I'll fold it during the game."

I roll my eyes and shove my brother. "You're such a momma's boy."

Leo just smiles even bigger. "Yup. You trying to tell me you don't want Jax to be a momma's boy one day?"

Well . . . damn. I hadn't thought about it like that. And now that I am, I guess I do . . . Because at some point, I'm going to become his mom.

By the time the game starts, Jax is asleep in a crib mom put in the guest room upstairs—because she's crazy like that—and Kerrigan is falling asleep on the couch. The kids are great with bedtime, and that's usually seven o'clock, which was an hour ago. I probably should have just watched the game alone, but I'm not sure I could have done it.

"Honey, you could put Kerrigan in your old bed. I haven't gotten a toddler bed yet because I wasn't sure if she was in one or if she was in a twin."

"Mom, you didn't have to do all this," I tell her as I pull the blanket up around Kerrigan.

"I know I didn't, but I wanted to. This is your family, Everly. And that makes them *our* family. Take it from someone who didn't have family when I met the Sinclairs. You can never have too many people who love and accept and support you. Let me spoil my first grandchildren."

"Mom," my voice shakes, and Dad hisses.

"Don't make her cry, Annabelle."

"Shush, Dec. A mother's job is to make their daughters cry," she tells him.

I shake my head. "Pretty sure it's not, Mom."

"Cross is back on the ice," Tommy says as he leans forward and starts rattling off Cross's statistics.

"Is he going after the puck or the player?" Dad asks as he watches Cross get away with high-sticking number two on the Pittsburgh team. Damn it.

"That's no player," Leo says, and I throw an elbow his way. "That's Everly's ex-boyfriend."

Cross slams him into the boards behind the net, where Jace Kingston is. It looks like Keith gets caught in Jace's stick, and that's when the God of War wreaks havoc. Ares throws down his gloves and punches Keith, then yanks his hockey jersey over his head so Keith can't fight back.

Oh my God.

Cross moves Ares out of the way and takes his shot, and all the players fly off the benches as a team-wide fight breaks out.

"What the hell?" Dad asks.

"Shit. Why do I think that's my fault?" Leo asks.

"It's not," I tell him. "It's not even *my* fault."

I hadn't thought about how I'm supposed to get the kids out of the car when they're both asleep and I'm by myself until it happened tonight. I look at my back seat, then at the kids. I don't want to leave one back there while I carry the other in. And I don't want to wake either of them up.

Shit.

Jax's car seat is heavy when it's hanging from the bend of your damn arm, but I've got it, and I'm so damn proud of myself when I manage to get Kerrigan on my hip without her waking up. That is, until I get to the door and realize I have no possible hope of reaching my house keys.

Fuck my life.

By the time Cross gets home, the kids are asleep in bed, and I'm sitting on the couch, crying. Sobbing may be more accurate. He comes in and dumps his hockey bag in the mudroom, then moves next to me. "Hey, baby. What's wrong?"

"I couldn't figure out what to do about the kids," I cry.

"What's wrong with the kids?" he asks, fear lacing his tone.

I shake my head wildly. "Nothing. Nothing is wrong. But they were both asleep, and I didn't want to wake either of them up to bring them inside. And I didn't want to leave either of them outside while I brought the other one in because if they woke up alone, they'd be scared, and what if some crazy person came and stole them out of the driveway. And then I couldn't reach my keys. And Leo said Jax was gonna be a momma's boy, and he meant I was gonna be his momma. And my mom went on a shopping spree so our kids could have everything they ever wanted at her house. Seriously, she's better than Santa." I pause and wipe my eyes, smiling a little when I think about getting to spoil the kids and wake up with them on Christmas morning. "We're so screwed in a few months."

"You said our kids, baby," Cross whispers with awe filling his voice. He pulls me onto his lap and moves my hair out of my face. "You called them *our* kids."

"Well, they are our kids. And when that clicked, so did something else, you big pain in my ass." I smack his big chest.

"Hey. Can we back up to you happy crying because Jaxon's going to be a momma's boy and you're going to be his momma?" His hand cups my jaw and pulls me toward him. "Because those may be my new favorite words."

"No. We cannot go back to that, Cross. What you did tonight was stupid. And irresponsible. And you or Ares could have gotten hurt. One of your teammates could have gotten hurt."

"The only one who got hurt was Dolan, baby." A smile stretches across his handsome face, and I cringe. "I heard a rumor he had to go to the hospital."

"Cross . . . stop. I don't think that's funny," I scold, then grab his wrist, needing to be anchored to him when I say this. "I need you to go with me tomorrow to see my parents."

"Is everything okay?"

"Something clicked tonight, somewhere between Leo's momma's boy joke and Kerrigan having a tea party with my mom and Uncle Tommy. And it got cemented when I couldn't figure out how to get them both safely in the house at the same time. If heaven forbid, something ever happened to either one of them, I'd want to know. I'd need to know. Because I'd want to slay all their dragons for them. And if either of them ever came to us and told us something awful happened to them, I'd hope they'd go to the police and report it so that person who did it could be punished."

"Baby . . ."

"I'd like you to take me to my parents' tomorrow morning. Then I'd like to go to the police department." A heavy weight feels like it's crushing my chest, but there's a hope there too. One I'm trusting to push away the weight after tomorrow.

"I'll hold your hand every single step of the way, Everly."

I close my eyes and nod. "No running."

"Never again." Cross presses his lips to mine, and I lay my head on his chest and listen to the heavy beat of his heart.

"I don't want to wait until June to marry you, Cross."

"I'll print you a schedule tomorrow. Pick a Saturday we don't have a game and tell me where to be, baby. I'll do whatever you want. I just need you, Kerrigan, and Jax."

"And our families. We have to have them. Lindy's mom is an event planner. Once we get a date, she'll make it magical."

"It already is." Cross's heart beats steady and strong against my cheek, and I thank God for magic because I think he was my birthday wish come true.

𝔗𝔥𝔢 𝔓𝔥𝔦𝔩𝔩𝔶 𝔓𝔯𝔢𝔰𝔰

KROYDON KRONICLES

BREAKING NEWS

Keith Dolan, formerly of the Pittsburg Pythons hockey team, was convicted today on three counts of aggravated sexual assault in the first degree, and two additional counts of aggravated sexual assault in the second degree. He's been sentenced to forty years in a maximum security prison. With the chance for parole after thirty years. He will be on parole supervision for life as a registered sex offender. The first woman of the five women who came forward, Ms. Everly Wilder, said that she was grateful that this predator was off the streets and that he could no longer hurt another woman. She thanked her husband for giving her the strength to come forward.

#KroydonKronicles

EPILOGUE

"It's hard to believe it's been a year," I say to my husband as we walk along the sandy beach at our family's Jersey Shore compound, which Cross added to a month ago when we bought a house here too. Jax is chasing Kerrigan, who's flying a beautiful butterfly kite that Aunt Nattie and Uncle Brady bought her for her birthday last week. Our girl is really into butterflies at the moment.

"Best year of my life, wife." He pulls my hand up to his lips and kisses my rings.

"Yeah. It's been a pretty good one." I smile when Jax's chubby legs move faster than his little body can keep up with, and he tumbles into the sand. When Kerrigan turns around to make sure he's okay, he throws sand in her face, and she ends up in tears.

"Fucking terrible twos," Cross groans, and I laugh.

"He's barely a year and a half."

Kerrigan comes running over, followed by Jax, and I look at my husband. "Tell me again how it's just two-year-olds."

THE WILDCAT

A few hours later, the kids are in bed, and the group of us are sitting around a big teak table on our back deck that overlooks the bay. Our small-ish circle has grown. What used to be the five of us girls and Callen and Maddox now includes Easton and Griffen, and Cross, Kerrigan and Jax. Not to mention Bellamy and Caitlin, as well as Ares and at least Leo, if not Hendrix too.

Once Nixon graduated, he moved back home, so he's been around more since May. And last week, he was drafted to the Revolution. They needed a new center since Jace Kingston retired.

The Revolution won the Stanley Cup this year, and Cross was the top scorer on the team again. It's been an incredible ride, and I didn't miss a single game.

"Earth to blondie." Ares snaps his fingers in front of my face. "You suck at poker. You know that, right?"

"Kiss my ass, God of War. I believe that's a royal flush." I lay down my cards and watch the confidence fall from his cocky face. "You owe me two nights of babysitting, starting tonight." I laugh and push up from the chair and jump for Cross to catch me.

"Hey . . . I never said tonight," Ares calls out as Cross walks us around the other side of the deck, then down the steps and out onto the sand.

"You think the kids will still be alive when we get back?" Cross asks with such a devious grin.

"Your brother is more than capable of keeping the kids alive. But Lindy and Easton are staying with us, so really, she's the one babysitting, and I only need a few minutes alone with you, big man."

"Give me ten minutes, and I'll get you off twice."

"We're on the beach at eleven o'clock at night, Cross. We may not have ten minutes. Make them count."

I giggle when he tosses me over his shoulder. My long sundress catches in the breeze and covers his face, so he can't see as he stumbles over to the lifeguard stand—that gets moved back by the dunes every day at six p.m.—and lays me back against the ladder.

"How fast do we need it, Cinderella?"

His hand is under my dress and inside my panties before the question even leaves his mouth.

"Hmm . . . Keep doing that, and I'll only need three minutes. Four, tops."

And it's true. Not only is Cross Wilder father of the year, an incredible husband, and the captain of the Philadelphia Revolution, my favorite title for him happens to be sex god. Because what this man does to me is absolutely otherworldly.

My hands move to the belt of his cargo shorts at the same time he boosts me up and pulls my dress up with me. "Three minutes left, baby," he murmurs against my ear as he shoves my panties aside and impales me on his hard cock.

I wrap my arms and legs around him and let him take all the weight as he fucks me like I weigh absolutely nothing.

"Oh God, Cross," I cry out, then laugh when we hear a voice not far away.

"Come fast, Cinderella, before we get caught. Come now, and I'll fuck that ass in the dead of night when everyone else in our house is fast asleep. Come now, and I'll stuff that pussy full of my fingers and that ass full of my cock, and make you forget anyone besides the two of us even exists."

And when I scream and come, Cross fills me up on a long groan before he drops my feet to the ground and shoves his dick back in his shorts. He takes my hand in his, and runs with me, laughing all the way back to our house.

"Back so soon, you two love birds?" Brynlee asks.

"I can just see the headline now." Lindy dramatically runs her hand through the air above her head like she's reading a marquee. "Kroydon Hills power couple, Cross and Everly Wilder, caught with sand in their ass after a quick fuckfest on the Longport beach."

Maddox chokes on his beer until Caitlin pounds a fist on his back. "Breathe, big brother. It's not like we all haven't had sex on that beach."

"What the actual fuck, Cait?"

Nixon shakes his head. "Welcome to my hell."

"Fuck off, little brother." I laugh. "Maybe if you got your own sex life, you wouldn't be so concerned with mine."

"It's a good sex life." Cross hands me a glass of wine.

"It's a great sex life," I agree.

"Oh my God. Stop. I'm begging you, evil twin. Please. You two are worse than Mom and Dad," Hendrix pleads, and I've got to say, I now consider being compared to my parents a compliment. I hope I'm still banging Cross's brains out in an outdoor shower when we're forty-five the way they got caught earlier today.

"What did I tell you about the evil twin shit?" Cross glares at Hendrix, who takes a step back.

"Right. Sorry. Old habits die hard," Hendrix groans.

I tap my wine glass against Cross's beer bottle. "It's a good life."

"It's a great life."

"Cocky," I tease, just to hear him say . . .

"Arrogance, baby. This is arrogance."

I fucking love his arrogance.

The End

. . .

Want more Everly & Cross?
Download their extended epilogue here!

Download the extended epilogue here

NOTE TO THE READER

Unfortunately, I think so many of us have experienced something similar to what Everly went through at some point in our lives. I know that I have, and that experience shaped this book in a way I never saw coming when I was working on the original plot and outline.

One in every six American women has been the victim of an attempted or completed rape in her lifetime.

If you or anyone you know is a victim of sexual assault, or rape please reach out. You are not alone.

National Sexual Assault Hotline: 1-800-656-4673

The Philly Press

KROYDON KRONICLES

NOT READY TO SAY GOODBYE YET?

Looks like our favorite Kroydon Hills socialites are at it again. Baby Kingston and the blonde bombshell both got their happily ever afters, now is the good twin, Grace Sinclair, looking to settle down too?

The Knockout, Grace's book, is releasing April 25th.

Preorder The Knockout Now

#KroydonKronicles #TheKnockout

WHAT COMES NEXT?

If you haven't read the first book in the Kings Of Kroydon Hills series, you can start with All In today!

Read All In for FREE on KU

ACKNOWLEDGMENTS

M. ~ Every word I write is because you're my strength.

My dream team, Brianna and Heather ~ Thank you for all that you do to keep my world spinning while I hide in my cave and get lost in Kroydon Hills. I am forever grateful.

Dena ~ We did it! I keep saying one of these days I will get back on schedule. Here's hoping it happens with the next book.

To the incredible women who read every word many, many, many times before this book was ready to be published, Jenn, Tammy, Bri, Heather, Vicki, & Kelly ~ Thank you from the very bottom of my heart. I am so lucky to have you in my corner and to count you as my friends.

For all of my Jersey Girls ~ Thank you for giving me a safe space and showing me so much grace.

To all of the Indie authors out there who have helped me along the way – you are amazing! This community is so incredibly supportive, and I am so lucky to be a part of it.

Thank you to all of the bloggers who took the time to read, review, and promote The Wildcat.

And finally, the biggest thank you to you, the reader. To

those of you who have been with me since Everly's parents' book was published three years ago and those of you have just stumbled onto the world of Kroydon Hills now, I hope you've enjoyed reading Everly and Cross as much as I have loved writing them.

ABOUT THE AUTHOR

Bella Matthews is a USA Today & Amazon Top 50 Bestselling author. She is married to her very own Alpha Male and raising three little ones. You can typically find her running from one sporting event to another. When she is home, she is usually hiding in her home office with the only other female in her house, her rescue dog Tinker Bell by her side. She likes to write swoon-worthy heroes and sassy, smart heroines. Sarcasm is her love language and big family dynamics are her favorite thing to add to each story.

Stay Connected

Amazon Author Page: https://amzn.to/2UWU7Xs
Facebook Page: https://www.facebook.com/bella.matthews.3511
Reader Group: https://www.facebook.com/groups/599671387345008/
Instagram: https://www.instagram.com/bella.matthews.author/
Bookbub: https://www.bookbub.com/authors/bella-matthews
Goodreads: https://www.goodreads.com/.../show/20795160.Bella_Matthews
TikTok: https://vm.tiktok.com/ZMdfNfbQD/
Newsletter: https://bit.ly/BMNLsingups
Patreon: https://www.patreon.com/BellaMatthews

ALSO BY BELLA MATTHEWS

Kings of Kroydon Hills
All In
More Than A Game
Always Earned, Never Given
Under Pressure

Restless Kings
Rise of the King
Broken King
Fallen King

The Risks We Take Duet
Worth The Risk
Worth The Fight

Defiant Kings
Caged
Shaken
Iced
Overruled
Haven

Playing To Win
The Keeper
The Wildcat
The Knockout (coming soon)

The Sweet Spot (coming soon)

CHECK OUT BELLA'S WEBSITE

Scan the QR code or go to http://authorbellamatthews.com to stay up to date with all things Bella Matthews

Printed in Great Britain
by Amazon